MIKE AND MADDIE MYSTERIES

VOLUME 1

DAISY LANDISH

Editing by Rachael Lammie
Cover by Daisy Landish

BEACHES AND TRAILS
PUBLISHING

ABOUT THE AUTHOR

Daisy Landish is a romance and cozy mystery author living in the UK, whose clean and sweet stories have tugged at readers' heartstrings across the pond and beyond. When she's not writing love stories, Daisy spends her time reading, hiking at dawn, and riding into the sunset on her horse, Rosebud.

Join Daisy's Newsletter for updates and giveaways!
www.daisylandishromance.com

f facebook.com/daisylandishromance

X x.com/daisy_landish

⊙ instagram.com/beachesandtrailspublishing

a amazon.com/author/daisylandish

BB bookbub.com/authors/daisy-landish

g goodreads.com/Daisy_Landish

ALSO BY DAISY LANDISH

Clean Regency Romance

The Lady Series - The Allington Collection

The Lady Series - The Gillingham Collection

The Lady Series - The Blackmore Collection

Clean Contemporary Romance

Love on Spruce Island

Second Chance

Cherry Tree Island

The Wedding Trio

Extra Credit

Clean Contemporary Western Romance

Counting on a Cowboy

Focusing on the Cowboy

Cozy Mysteries

Jane and Kennedy Daniels Mysteries

Pine Grove Mysteries

Annie Archer Paranormal Mysteries

Wilma Wade Holiday Mysteries

Mike and Maddie Mysteries

Clean Holiday Romance

The Yuletide Thief

Grounded at Christmas

Clueless at Christmas

Christmas Surprise

Mistletoe Magic

CONTENTS

ON THIN ICE

A LITTLE FROSTY

A BAD EGG

TAKING THE FALL

MURDER AT THE RETREAT

ON THIN ICE

CHAPTER
ONE

MADELEINE "MADDIE" Moreau curled her legs beneath her as she took her seat on the couch, facing her two friends. The cup of coffee warmed her hands as she nodded at Detective Carson Luttrell.

"I hope I'm not interrupting anything," Carson said. He leaned back in the white suede chair, crossing his legs. A beam of sunlight fell from the open windows onto his shoulder, illuminating the shiny pin on his lapel.

"Not at all," Maddie said. "Mike and I were just going over my publicity plan for the latest novel I'm writing. But I have to admit I was getting bored and frustrated with it."

Michael "Mike" Malison, sitting on the other end of the couch, chuckled. "I could tell. So, Carson. What's wrong?"

A wry smile flickered across Carson's face. He turned his mug of coffee around in his hands, the sunlight highlighting the strands of gray creeping into his dark, curly hair. His brown eyes darkened as his nostrils flared. All clear indications he was avoiding the conversation.

Hmmm. Maddie glanced over at Mike, who quirked a single eyebrow at him. This meant something juicy was happening. Carson never hemmed and hawed over his words unless a case was involved.

It was just the sort of distraction Maddie was looking for. Usually, her day job working as a plotter for other writers kept her busy enough. She loved writing, but she truly enjoyed creating the characters and stories. Once it got to writing the same characters day after day, she lost interest and got bored.

Unfortunately, Maddie got bored quickly.

"Oh, come on, Carson," she wheedled. "It's about that diamond heist, isn't it? Do you need our help on the case?"

Carson shot her a dirty look. She only smiled back. At thirty years old, she was more mature than when they had met; him a thirty-five-year-old police officer who had just made detective, her a twenty-year-old writer who had just moved into her penthouse suite in Coeur D'Alene, Idaho.

When she was robbed, she met then-nineteen Mike, and they gently inserted themselves into the investigation. Ultimately, they helped Carson bust a larger thieving ring than he realized he was facing.

Over the last ten years, the three of them had gotten rather good at working together. Unofficially, of course.

Maddie pushed the sleeves of her oversized sweater to her elbows and waited.

"I'm at a dead end," Carson finally confessed. There was a sour note to his voice; he didn't like to admit when he needed to ask for help with a case. "I thought maybe you two could give me some insights I've missed so far."

"Always glad to help," Mike said. He sipped his coffee, his dark eyes locked on Carson with a gleeful glint.

Maddie smirked. Mike would never admit it, but he was itching for something new and exciting. The long Idaho winter was just ending, and they could finally go outside without wearing a million layers. Time to break out of the encapsulating snow and ice and have an adventure.

Oh, I've got to remember that one, she thought.

Carson cleared his throat. "You listening?"

Maddie snapped back to attention. What had he been saying? Right. Someone had stolen two pounds of uncut diamonds from the airport, and the investigation had stopped when he uncovered a single diamond on the floor of an ice factory.

"As I was saying," Carson continued, "since that single diamond was reported, I have uncovered no further leads. Of course, the factory owner hasn't made it easy. Mrs. Lark has been acting like she's dealing with classified material."

"I'm sure that the motels and gas stations that buy ice from the factory value their privacy," Mike noted with a wry grin.

Maddie chuckled. "I've got it. Lark made a deal with the diamond dealer who imported the gems. They planned out the perfect theft and hid the uncut diamonds in ice so that they could transport it all around the country."

"What for?" Mike asked. "If they're the dealer's diamonds, why would he want to steal them from himself?"

"Insurance. Then all they have to do is buy back those bags, and voila!" She clutched her coffee with one hand as she swept her other arm out. "They have both the insurance money, they sell the diamonds on the black market, and they build a new factory in the Sahara to make ice and make a killing in profits."

Carson pinched the bridge of his nose.

"Why the Sahara?" Mike asked. "It would cost more to transport the water there to make the ice than it would transport just the ice."

Madeline tapped her chin. "Good point. Maybe they're secret environmentalists and want to make an ice factory in Antarctica to combat global warming?"

"Eh... not realistic with the heat a factory would put off," Mike shook his head.

"Can I finish?" Carson asked. Though his tone was severe, he clearly struggled to keep from smiling.

Maddie smirked and nodded at him to continue.

"Anyway, I have had nothing new in the case, and I just keep coming back to that factory. I'm getting pressure to drop it and get on with something else." A flash of annoyance crossed Carson's face.

Mike leaned forward, frowning deeply. "They want you just to give up? Even though it's only been a few days?"

"Two pounds of diamonds aren't what they used to be," Carson said dryly.

"But if you close the case, the thieves will get away with it," Mike argued.

"I know."

Maddie hummed. "We can't be certain what their motives are, either. It was a brazen theft, and anyone who could get the diamonds so quickly and easily had a reason to do so. For all we know, they're part of some vast criminal organization using the money to make it harder to weed them out. Or maybe they're some sort of Bond villains who will blow up Spokane."

Carson sighed. "I don't think you can blow up Spokane with diamonds."

"Not directly, no. But my point is that we don't know what they will do with these diamonds. I don't care if your captain thinks it wastes time. We need to find them."

"And that's why I'm here." Carson finished his coffee. "Because I can't give my full attention to this case anymore, I'm hoping you two will work some of your magic. Can I count on you?"

Mike set his coffee aside and stood. "Of course. We know the thieves took the diamonds to the ice factory. It's a good guess that they froze the gems in ice to ship them out without raising suspicions. Have you gotten the factory's sale records?"

Carson pulled his briefcase onto his lap and opened it. He handed a file to Mike. "They've made hundreds of deliveries since the theft. I would need an army to check out every single place that bought ice from them. Even if I shut it all down right now so I could investigate every purchase—"

"The cost of reimbursing lost revenue from those businesses would sink the Coeur D'Alene police force," Maddie finished.

"And in the meantime, it is possible that the bags of ice that contain the diamonds have already been taken. I'll have cost the department and hundreds of businesses a lot of money for no reward," Carson agreed.

Mike closed the file and shook his head. "All right. So that's not a good plan of action. We could put it out online for people to be aware."

"And nine times out of ten, I'd say the average person is going to hand over the diamonds if they found them," Carson said, "but it's that one out of ten who would actually look for them."

"Not to mention it's unlikely that the thieves would have hidden the diamonds without a way to retrieve them," Maddie added.

Her shoulders slumped. No, there would be no wild road trip across the country, hitting every motel and gas station they came across. Shame. That would be quite an adventure.

She rested her pointed chin on her palm as she looked out the window. From this angle, she could see the long, beautiful lake the city built along. The city was tiny compared to Vancouver, Canada, where she was born, but this place had a charm she couldn't get enough of.

With a sigh, she shook her head. "It just occurred to me we don't even know if the thieves hid the diamonds in the ice or if they just stopped in the ice factory just because it was empty and offered a place to hide from the police."

"Or, if they hid the diamonds in the ice, they could have taken the entire block with them. There's no way to track where each block was sent or if there are any missing," Mike offered.

Carson crossed his legs and nodded at them. "And now you know why I'm stumped."

"Yeah," Maddie fought, a growing grin on her face. It was just the sort of enigma she loved to face.

But her grin faded away when she saw the bitter disappointment on Carson's face. "The more I think about this case, the more I think those diamonds are lost. Forever."

CHAPTER
TWO

CARSON STARED into his empty coffee mug, his shoulders tense and his brow furrowed. The last thing he wanted to do was to just give up on this case. If his two young friends couldn't give him any new insights, he might not have a choice.

"Well, I don't think sitting around will help anything," Mike said, taking Carson's empty mug.

Maddie offered her mug to him as well. "We don't have anywhere to start just yet."

"Then let's go for a walk and discuss things more; we've been sitting around long enough, and it's a lovely day out," Mike advised.

Carson glanced outside at the sunny day. Because of the long lake Coeur D'Alene was built along, the weather here was milder than in other places in the state. But winters still seemed to last forever. He loved the look of fresh snow, but dealing with the ice and cold was getting more difficult as he got older.

"A nice walk sounds like a good idea," he agreed.

Maddie let out a long groan but nodded as she said, "Let me get changed first."

Soon enough, they were walking along a stone path along the lake. The water was blue and clear today, the ice and snow at the edges of the shore melting to almost nothing. The air was still, allowing the warmth of the sunlight to fall on them.

"We can safely assume that the diamonds were taken to the ice factory on purpose," Mike said as the three walked side by side. "It makes the most sense. They are easier to hide and transport. It's more logical than the thieves finding the factory open and empty."

"Agreed," Maddie and Carson said together.

Maddie let out a bell-like laugh and nudged him with her elbow. "Jinx."

Carson smiled and rolled his eyes. "You know that doesn't work on me."

"Ah, well. Do you have any suspects in the factory workers? It has to be someone who knows how to use the equipment to freeze the ice and where everything is. So, either the thieves have someone on the inside, or they've worked at other factories." She paused, and Carson could almost see her imagination taking off on her. "Or—"

"Let's stick to reality, shall we?" Carson interrupted.

Usually, he found Maddie's theatrical scenarios quite charming. There had even been a few times when it led them to the right clues. However, with his worries already so prevalent in his mind, he didn't have the patience for the stories.

Maddie blushed but nodded. "I'll stick with the case rather than fantasies; I doubt the Snow Queen has anything to do with this."

"Regarding your question, no. I don't have any suspects." Carson shook his head as a gull wheeled about overhead, crying out. He rolled his shoulders, trying to loosen the tension there. "I've looked at their employment records. There have been no new hires at the plant in a few decades."

"Decades?" Mike questioned, turning the collar of his peacoat up as a rush of wind came across the lake. Maddie shivered and squeezed herself between the two men.

Carson took off his scarf—he was a little warm, despite the wind, and handed it to Madeleine. "They're all over the retirement age, and the few I talked with said that the pay was good and there was enough to keep them busy without it being too much responsibility. They talked about just making sure the machines ran and calling in mechanics if there were any problems."

Maddie frowned at that. "There has to be someone who moves the ice blocks around and loads trucks and whatnot. There has to be physical labor involved that would be too much day in and out for people in their seventies and eighties."

"I agree; this is suspicious," Mike said.

Carson stepped around the evidence that a dog-walker had come by without a poop bag, then sighed. "I looked at things. It all seems automated, and the transportation drivers do the heavy lifting you were talking about."

"Aha!" Maddie crowed, coming to a stop. "That's it! The transport drivers—do you have a list of them?"

Carson shook his head silently. "I was told they were subcontractors. I've been stonewalled at every attempt to get that information."

"It has to be one of them, though," Maddie said. "I can't imagine that an old person could move around a heavy block of ice, let alone lose one. Whenever I visit my grandmother, she knows where exactly everything is at all times. Not to mention, they would have to wait around for it to thaw out."

"There are many different ways to speed up the thawing process," Carson argued.

"True. But if they're all in their seventies and older, wouldn't they just be too impatient?"

Carson had to laugh. "Oh, Madeleine, not all the elderly are like your grandmother. Doesn't it make sense that someone with almost limitless time on their hands would simply wait for it to melt, as opposed to someone under a time crunch?"

Mike cleared his throat. "Carson has a point. Anyone would have the same problem. They'd all have to wait for the ice to melt."

"How long does it take to thaw out something that size?" Maddie asked.

Mike shook his head. "At room temperature? What if they turned the heat up in the room it was in? If they poured boiling water over it? Or smashed it down first?"

"That is an excellent point." Maddie started walking again,

Carson's scarf wrapped around her neck even though the brief wind had died.

Carson sighed. "It appears we aren't any closer to finding out who did it."

"I disagree," Mike said swiftly as he adjusted his leather gloves. As usual, he looked as though he was expecting his picture to be put on the cover of a magazine. "We have, in fact, decided we need to learn about the transportation workers."

"And how did we do that?" Carson asked dryly.

"Because the heavy lifting had to be done by someone. And no matter how well they work out, it's doubtful any person over seventy will lift that weight. And how would they transport the ice?"

Maddie lifted a hand, swirling her finger in the air as though she were drawing it out. "If it were me, I would break it down at the ice plant and then take it home with me in a rubber tub of some sort and then put it in my shower with a fine cheesecloth over the drain so as not to lose any diamonds, and turn the water on hot to melt it quickly."

Mike frowned. "Ah. Yes, that puts our elderly workers back on the suspect lists."

"No, it doesn't," Carson said quickly. "Why hide it in a block of ice if they were just going to destroy that ice at the factory itself?"

"Of course." Mike smacked his forehead. "Which means we can eliminate the possibility that they took these diamonds home, either. Why would they? No. The ice was for secret transport, which brings us back to the transport workers."

"And then," Carson said, "there's the diamond that was called in. No thief capable of pulling off a heist would be so careless. I wonder if maybe it was left to lead a false rail."

"Or the thief isn't as professional as we've assumed," Maddie said.

Carson frowned at her. Her tone was suggesting something. "But they could still pull off that heist."

"If we're talking a transport driver, they could have been the same driver who was supposedly robbed in the first place," she pointed out.

Carson's gaze darkened. Of course. Even though the truck driver was among the suspects in the original heist, he hadn't looked for any connection to the ice factory. An oversight that would soon be corrected.

"Or there was an amateur partner who butted in after the fact," Mike said.

"All this speculation isn't helping with this case." Carson turned back toward the head of the path. "We won't learn more until we have gone to the next step. So, I will return to the ice factory to get a list of the transport workers."

Mike nodded once. "And see if you can get a list of any ice blocks that have been lost. I'll make some calls and see if I can determine if any of their clients didn't get the amount of ice they were looking for."

"Thank you."

"And me?" Maddie asked as she pulled deeper into her coat; the wind had picked up again, biting with more frost.

Carson ran a hand through his hair. "I want you to go undercover. See if you can get some information Angela Lark would never tell a cop."

Maddie grinned. "With pleasure."

CHAPTER
THREE

ANGELA LARK'S over-glossed lips pinched into a scowl as she held the manilla file folder out to Carson. Today he was dressed in a buttoned-up suit, the sort he always wore when investigating.

"Thank you, Mrs. Lark," he said, tucking the file under his arm. "Your cooperation will be noted."

Angela rolled her eyes and folded her thin arms across her chest. "Thank goodness for that. You think that my factory had something to do with it. It's beyond tiresome. I don't even think you found a genuine diamond on my floor; you're just making things up."

Making things up? Carson kept his gaze steady. She was nervous. Her lips kept twitching, and her attempts at deflection only made it more obvious.

"I just want things to get back to normal. Is that so bad?" she whined. "None of my employees would do something like this. They've been working here for twenty years! Why would people so loyal get involved in criminal activity?"

"You must treat your employees very well to have such low turnover."

"I do," Angela said, that twitch to her lips getting even more pronounced. She shifted her weight from side to side as she pointed at

the folder. "The company I outsource for the deliveries hires the transport workers. They have nothing to do with me."

Carson smiled, keeping his demeanor calm. He didn't want to
spook her if Angela Lark was involved in this somehow. "Oh, of
course. We're investigating the possibility that one or more drivers
could have been involved and taken advantage of your factory."

Her shoulders loosened slightly.

"Especially with such an elderly population of employees," he
added.

She tensed once more and looked away. "Well, I'll admit that sometimes the transport drivers get a little too friendly, but that's because
they see my workers like grandparents. Nothing to do with sneaking
about the factory and breaking the rules."

"Of course not."

"My people have worked hard their entire lives. They've earned
the right to have jobs where they don't have to do all that much and
still receive better pay than what they could get from their pensions."

"Twenty years is a long time to work at one place," Carson noted.

"Employee loyalty is important to me and all my workers." Angela
narrowed her eyes at him, lifting her chin slightly as though daring
him to say otherwise.

An odd reaction to such a simple statement, Carson thought. While
the two looked over the transport worker's list, he noted to share these
details with Mike.

He opened his mouth to continue, but a knock on the door interrupted him.

"Enter," Angela called a little too quickly.

Her receptionist, Brandon, a young man, stuck his head through
the door. "Mrs. Lark, your appointment is here. Shall I show her in?"

Angela's eyes darted to Carson. He could see how much she
wanted just to say yes and have him go away, but to her credit, she
didn't. Instead, she gave him a questioning look, leaving it up to him.

Carson smiled once more and lifted the file. "I have what I need,
Mrs. Lark. Thank you once again. I'll take my leave now."

As he headed out toward the parking lot, his eyes briefly met those
of Angela's next appointment. He nodded politely in greeting.

Maddie turned up her nose and folded her arms.

Carson bit back a chuckle. Maddie always loved getting into character when she went undercover. He hoped she would be more successful than he was.

As he headed out, Carson heard Brandon say, "Mrs. Lark will see you now," and he grinned. Everything was going according to plan.

MADDIE WAITED, her foot bouncing as she sat in the uncomfortable chair facing the receptionist's desk. Though she had scheduled her appointment for a half-hour later, she wanted to appear eager, so she came in early.

The waiting area was lavishly decorated with a thick carpet underfoot and expensive art on the walls. As her gaze skimmed over the paintings, she cocked her head. The only noise in the room was the faint buzzing of the lights and the whirling fan in the computer on the receptionist's desk.

She would never have suspected it from this room if she didn't know this was a factory. The equipment was noticeably quiet, and these walls had excellent soundproofing.

Maddie was inclined to believe it was the latter. This meant there could be a great deal behind those walls that she didn't know about. The workers themselves wouldn't be able to hear much, either.

She wanted to know why a factory would go through the effort of making everything so silent in the next room. And why would they put in all that money for the soundproofing? She once lived in an apartment that had a newborn baby above her. It was far cheaper to move than to renovate enough, so she was no longer hearing the crying at three in the morning.

A few minutes after Carson walked out, the soft thudding of heels on a carpet reached Maddie's ears. She turned to see Brandon slip back to his desk as a tall, stately woman with graying brown hair and a generous smile strode toward her.

"Miss Moreau, I'm so sorry to keep you waiting," Angela Lark said as she extended a hand.

"It's no problem at all." Maddie fluidly stood and shook Angela's hand. "And please, call me Madeleine."

She gathered her purse, smoothed the front of her tailored business suit, and followed Angela back to her office. The place was professionally decorated. Everything matched perfectly and was so put-together and clean that Maddie thought either Angela was an interior decorator or she had someone come in regularly to keep the look updated.

"Take a seat," Angela offered, gesturing to an all-white coach that had just come onto the market last week.

"Thank you, Mrs. Lark," Maddie said as she sat and crossed her ankles.

"Angela, please. I like to have a personal touch with my clients." Angela gave her a wide, winning smile as she stepped to her desk. "Would you like anything to drink? Tea? Coffee?"

"Tea, please. Orange pekoe if you have it."

Angela nodded once and started busying herself.

"Once again, I would like to apologize for your wait. I had some business to take care of, a client who had issues with another facility. He hoped we could quickly rectify the situation—which, of course, we can," Angela added, pouring the hot water into a mug.

Maddie waved a hand. "It's really no trouble at all."

Interesting that Angela was accommodating, despite the age difference, and Maddie's arrival so early. Was she just a good businesswoman? Or was there another reason behind it? She certainly seemed eager to put up a good front.

Would it work on people who didn't know Carson is a detective? Maddie wondered. She smiled and accepted the tea from Angela.

"Your office is beautiful," she said, holding the mug in both hands. "I must say, you look like you're doing very well for yourself. Forgive me if it's an intrusion, but is that a Gucci bag?"

"Oh, this?" Angela gestured to the purse on her desk and gave a little laugh.

Maddie nodded as she took a small sip of tea.

Angela picked up the bag and brushed off some imaginary lint. "It's beautiful, isn't it? Looks just like the real thing—but no. It's not

Gucci. It's one of those knock-off bags. See the stitching here? An obvious giveaway. I was terribly disappointed when I realized it."

"Oh, dear," Maddie pulled a sympathetic face. "I hope you didn't pay full price."

Angela made a dismissive noise as she fixed herself a mug of coffee. "No. The price should have been my first tipoff, but I guess I was just a little greedy."

Every brush stroke painted the picture a little clearer, and it was all wrong.

"I see."

Angela cleared her throat as she sat down. "Well. Shall we get to business? I understand you're opening an ice carving studio in Spokane, correct?"

Maddie nodded. "I ran a successful ice carving studio up in Vancouver and am looking to restart here. I already have clients lined up for a rather large wedding, but I can't say more. Confidentiality and all that."

"Of course," Angela nodded. "How much do you think you would need?"

"For this client? At least fifty blocks, minimum three feet by two feet. Can you provide that?"

"We're set up to create blocks of various sizes. And transportation is no problem, either. My factory delivers to five other states, so Spokane is no trouble."

"Excellent. And how often do you do deliveries that way?"

"Once a week."

Maddie nodded, making a note of that information. "My studio is rather small for the time being. Building up the clientele and reputation will take time. Unfortunately, this means I don't have a lot of storage space. Do you have anywhere here where I can store the sculptures?"

Angela beamed. "Ah! No need for that. I have a lovely storage space in Spokane that I use as a distribution warehouse."

"Oh? When I researched your facility online, I saw no sign of one."

"Well, I don't want to give away all my secrets to my competitors now, do I?"

"Makes sense," Maddie agreed. For tax evasion. I bet she produces much more ice than she reports and uses this warehouse as a shell company to hide it from the IRS.

"Yes. So, for a small fee, I could give you a space within the warehouse freezers to store your sculptures."

"That sounds lovely," Maddie nodded as she sipped her tea.

Carson wanted her to get a tour of the facility, so she could check on anything that was out of the ordinary – things Angela would hide from the police, not a client. The problem was, exactly how was she going to get this tour?

She didn't want to seem too eager, so she asked, "My orders won't get mixed up with other orders, will they?"

Angela shook her head. "There are several separate freezers. I have the same setup here, except on a smaller scale. Would you like to see it?"

Gotcha. Maddie schooled her expression so she didn't tip Angela off. "That would be wonderful, if you have the time."

Angela set her coffee aside and stood. "I always have time for my clients, Madeleine."

Maddie stood as well and slid her purse over her shoulder. "Thank you so much. It might sound silly, but mines and factories have always fascinated me. I'd like to see anything you can show me."

"Then let's get you a tour of the entire factory, shall we?" Angela said, putting her Gucci handbag in her desk drawer. "I think we are going to get along splendidly."

CHAPTER
FOUR

THE DAY BLUSTERED OUTSIDE—WINTER'S last raging charge against the coming spring. Inside the café, warm lights set off a homey glow that bolstered the patrons against the coming storm.

Mike scrawled the few lines on a napkin. He enjoyed writing whatever came to his mind, even if he would never use it. Since he had been waiting for Carson and Maddie for half an hour, he had amused himself by writing brief descriptions of the cafe and the people. He sat in their usual corner booth, far from anyone else.

He had worked in the café for almost a year while he was ghostwriting a series about restaurant staff. Never one to do less than his best, the owner still thought of him fondly. Mike loved the ambiance of the café and the possibilities of creating stories from the people he observed.

A cough pulled him from his thoughts, and he looked up to see Carson hang his coat on the hook at the end of the booth. The detective slid in, rubbings his hands together.

"Maddie hasn't gotten here yet, I see," Carson observed.

"No, not yet. I have ordered everyone's meals to be prepared as soon as we're all here—provided that you want the usual Salisbury steak?"

Carson belted out one of his signature booming laughs. "The day I don't get one of these delicious steaks is the day I'm put in the ground."

Mike chuckled, then straightened when Maddie walked into the café. The knitted beanie hid her chestnut brown hair while a scarf wound around her neck nearly covered half her face. She hurried over to them and slid in next to Carson.

"Sorry I'm late," she said as she took off her scarf. "The little corner store that I always go to fill up my car is closed. I know the owner was taking a trip somewhere, but I thought he would be back by now. I was almost empty by the time I got in line."

Mike steepled his fingers, leaning forward. "It's no problem. I already ordered our food—you want soup and the salmon fillet with chips?"

"You are the most wonderful man in the universe," Maddie sighed as she sunk into the booth.

"*Bien-sûr, mon cher*," he put on his best French accent—the latest hero in the book he was writing was French.

Maddie pursed her lips. "That's wrong."

"Is it?" Carson asked.

"*Mon* cher would be if he were addressing a man; I'm a woman, so it's *ma chérie*." Maddie took off her beanie and shook out her long hair. "You're going to have to do more research if you want your characters to be realistic."

Mike nodded seriously. "Perhaps you can give me some French lessons, then?"

"Depends on if you want France French or Quebecois. My tutor was from Quebec, and they have their own distinctive dialect."

The server headed over with two bowls of soup and one salad. He set the food down in front of them and pulled out the little notepad. "Can I get you anything else to drink?"

"The water is fine," Carson said.

"I'll have a peppermint tea," Maddie said.

The server nodded and glanced at Mike.

"Just water, thank you."

He headed off, and the three tucked into their first course. They didn't speak again until the server had brought Madeleine's tea over and left them to their meal. Then Carson speared through the lettuce of his salad and pushed it around the plate.

"I got the list of transport workers," he said. "I have little more than that to say. Madeleine, you can tell us how your meeting with Angela Lark went, and then Mike can report on what he found."

"*Je suis désolé,*" Mike said. "I must protest—I didn't find out anything useful. So, it's all down to Madeleine's undercover savvy."

Maddie sipped her soup off the spoon and glanced around. "I can tell you one thing. Angela Lark either has money to throw around, or she's so deep in debt that she'll drown in it."

"Oh?" Mike leaned forward. This was delightfully intriguing.

"She has a Gucci handbag that she tried to pass off as fake to me," Maddie said. "But trust me, I can tell a fake from a real. It had to have cost her at least fifteen thousand dollars."

Carson whistled.

Mike propped his chin on his hand. "Why would she try to make you think it's fake?"

"Because with everything else in that office? She is living far more than anything she can put on her taxes," Maddie replied. "She was overly accommodating to me while also being jaded; I guess she was concerned I might be from the IRS. The bag wasn't the only thing I spied as genuine that she tried to say was fake."

"And with her trying to make a good impression, there was really no reason for her to do that, except if she was suspicious," Carson said. His eyes darkened.

Mike knew the signs. "Ah, but even with her suspicions, she let things slip."

"Yeah, she did. She was still eager to make her sales even if she thought I might be fake." Maddie stirred her soup before catching herself and laying the spoon on the side. "She upsold everything that you can imagine."

Carson finished his salad, and Maddie pushed him the rest of her soup. By this time, it was old hat for them to do this. She just wanted enough to warm her up and tide her over, while Carson's salad wasn't nearly enough to satisfy his appetite for a man with that much muscle.

"As interesting as that is, did you get a tour?" Carson asked between bites of the soup.

"Yes. She was eager to show me around, actually," Maddie preened, flicking her hair behind her.

Carson nodded at her. "And?"

She scrunched up her nose, bringing the few freckles on it closer together. "I don't really know much about ice factories, but nothing seemed out of the ordinary with the machinery. She definitely has employees off the books. No way were they all retirees."

Mike finished his last spoonful of soup and leaned back, gently tapping the spoon against the rim of the bowl. "Did anything else stand out to you?"

"It was oddly quiet. Oh! And when she showed me the storage rooms," Maddie continued, straightening, "all the freezer doors were open except one. And it was also the only one with a lock on it."

"It would be very interesting to know what is in that freezer," Mike noted.

"Me, too," Maddie agreed. "But that's all I found out. I didn't dare ask about it. That felt like pushing my luck."

Carson grinned. The server came back, and they handed their dirty dishes to him and waited until they were alone again.

"Between the diamond on the floor and evidence that Angela is lying about her list of employees, I should have enough evidence to get a search warrant from Judge Wendell," he said. The hunter's glow was in his eyes. Clearly, he had locked in on something.

Maddie shivered as someone came through the café doors, bringing a gust of snow-tainted wind with them. "I hope you find something."

"I'm sure we will," Mike said. "Something that sets this case on a whole new angle."

He had no idea how accurate his prediction would be.

🐾

MIKE STARED AT CARSON, aghast. "A corpse?"

"His name was Willie Jayne," Carson said grimly. He had cast off his suit jacket and tie, and his hair was messed up. It was clear he'd been running his hands through it a lot today.

Maddie straightened the pile of board games on her kitchen table. "Well. It doesn't seem appropriate to have a game night after that news. A corpse in the freezer. I would never have suspected something like that!"

"I know." Carson leaned his elbows on the table, holding his head in his hands.

Mike understood. This case had just exploded. Missing diamonds was one thing. But to add murder to the mix? "So, who was this, Willie Jayne?"

Carson pushed a file over to him, not looking up. The poor guy was exhausted. It had to have been an endless day.

"Let's see what we have here." Mike opened the file, finding a long list of priors on the first page. He whistled. "This is an unusually long rap sheet. And is this his bank account?"

"Yes," Carson said.

Mike handed it to Maddie as he continued to look over the crimes they had arrested Willie Jayne for in the past.

Maddie hummed. "He recently came into money. But Angela Lark doesn't strike me as the killer type. Did you get anything out of her?"

"No. She was lawyered up before we found the body and wouldn't say a word to me or anyone else."

The wind shrieked outside as the day grew darker. Though nights were getting shorter, a storm made everything seem gloomy. The windows rattled with the force of the approaching weather front, and Mike rubbed his arms.

"If it starts snowing, can I sleep over?" he asked. Madeleine's apartment had two bedrooms and a comfortable pull-out sofa. There were plenty of times when he stayed with her when they were working on something together. "I walked," he added.

"Yeah, of course. With how it's looking out there, I was going to suggest you both stay the night. I have extra toothbrushes still," Madeline shuddered. "This weather makes me wish I were back in Vancouver. We never had storms like this."

They were all quiet for a moment before Mike cleared his throat. "I have to ask. How long was Willie Jayne in that freezer, and how did he die?"

CHAPTER
FIVE

CARSON STRAIGHTENED IN HIS CHAIR, feeling a heavy weight on his shoulders. He hated it when cases took these sorts of turns. Murder was never something he wanted to deal with; he especially hated it when a case he worked on with these two ended up including one.

Not that Maddie and Mike were all that young; Maddie was thirty, Mike twenty-nine. They weren't kids by any means. But there was still something about them that made Carson feel like a big brother. He wanted to look out for them.

Murderers were inherently dangerous in a way that put them at greater risk than poking around a diamond heist.

He knew they would not back down now that they were involved. These two might be eccentric with vivid imaginations. But one thing they were not was cowards or pushovers. He imagined that either of them could outlast a mule with their stubbornness.

"The autopsy is scheduled for tomorrow," he said, meeting their curious stares.

"What were your preliminary thoughts?" Mike pushed.

Carson couldn't help but smile wryly. If they were police officers, this intensity would serve them well. "I didn't see any sign of injury except for frostbite. I saw nothing that pointed to poison, either. But the body was covered in a thick layer of frost."

"Locking him into an air-tight freezer is a good way to murder someone," Mike said grimly.

"They're not airtight, though." Maddie propped her elbows against the table. "On my tour, they kept the storage area near freezing because the individual freezers weren't airtight. Angela said it was a safety precaution."

Carson frowned at her. "You didn't tell us this earlier."

"There wasn't a body earlier."

"Good point," Carson muttered.

"Angela also said that there were safety latches on the inside of the freezers to prevent people from getting stuck, as well as individual thermostats on the inside."

Carson absorbed that information as Mike started shooting off theories; he kept an ear to them, but none seemed quite right. As he churned over everything, something came to mind. He cleared his throat, and the other two fell silent.

"It was the only freezer with a lock on it; it could only be unlocked from the outside," he intoned. "There are also internal and external thermostats. If the internal one were disconnected, it would be fairly simple to kill someone by freezing him to death."

"Hypothermia," Mike murmured. "How low do the freezers get?"

"It was set to fourteen degrees."

Mike tapped his fingers against the table. "It would take less than an hour for him to suffer at those temperatures."

"The coroner estimated he'd been dead between ten and twelve hours."

Maddie shuddered as she shot up from the table. Carson jerked, his senses going on alert. But she only moved into the living room to grab one of her crocheted blankets to pull around her shoulders.

"I hate being cold," she said as she returned. "Just talking about this makes me hurt. I can't imagine what that poor man went through."

Mike turned Jayne's file to her. "He wasn't a poor man. He was a terrible criminal."

"All the same, if someone has to die, they don't deserve to suffer," Maddie said stoutly. She pulled the blanket tight around her thin shoulders and turned to Carson. "What else did you find?"

"Nothing. Not even ice. Certainly no diamonds."

"Well," Mike pushed back from the table. "This calls for wine, whiskey, and watermelon juice. I believe I left a few bottles here last time?"

"And they're right where you left them," Maddie said.

Mike made a tsking noise under his breath as he got the beverages and glasses. "What was the man wearing, anyway?"

Only Mike would care about how the dead man was dressed. Carson rubbed his forehead. "What does it matter?"

"We know Angela has employees that aren't on the list she gave you," Mike said as he poured Carson's whiskey.

"So?"

"So," he continued, "the clothes make the man—or in this case, tell us what he was there for."

Carson frowned.

Mike poured Maddie's watermelon juice and brought the drinks before returning for his wine. As he came back to settle at the table, he had that smug expression on his face. The one that said he'd worked something out but wanted to be asked about it so he could show off his brilliance.

Maddie indulged him. "How so?"

"If he wore clothing suitable for factory work, he was an unofficial employee. If he wasn't, then he didn't work at the factory. If he didn't work at the factory, he was there for another reason... his rap sheet includes fencing stolen jewelry." Mike grinned as he sipped his wine.

"Meaning he could have been the one that pulled off the heist," Maddie said, her expression brightening. "And then he arranged it with Angela to hide the diamonds at the factory. Only something went wrong, and she killed him."

Mike nodded once. "Depending on how he was dressed, of course."

Carson lifted his whiskey glass in congratulations. "He wasn't wearing the same clothes the others wear."

"Hot dog!" Maddie slapped the table with an open hand. "That has to be it, then! He didn't work at the factory."

"But then, that brings the question of how long he was locked in that freezer," Carson said quickly.

Mike nodded. "And why nobody heard him trying to get out."

Maddie swished her watermelon juice around in her cup. "I have an answer to that. That building was made to dampen sound at every level. You can't hear anything if you're not in the same room as the machinery. It must hold to the freezers as well."

"That is a good point." Mike sipped his wine and then set it aside, reaching for the file on Willie Jayne again.

He flipped through the papers. Carson leaned back in his chair, thinking their theory over. It made sense. "The only issue is how that diamond ended up on the factory floor. And what changed to make Angela lock Willie up."

Maddie gasped, making Carson jump again. She grabbed a paper from the folder and spun it around; it was a picture of Willie Jayne from his last arrest.

"This is Mr. Hodgens!"

Carson lifted an eyebrow. "Who?"

Maddie tapped the face in the picture. "He owns and manages the corner store gas station I always go to. Remember how yesterday I was late to the café because I couldn't fill up my car? It's him. No wonder he's been missing!"

Mike leaned close to Maddie, inspecting the picture. "She's right. That is certainly him."

As though things couldn't get any stranger! Carson ran a hand through his hair. "How long has he been managing the station?"

"Two, three years."

"So, he assumed a false identity to work in a gas station," Carson laughed as he pushed his whiskey away. He didn't feel like drinking. "How much do you want to bet that these diamonds aren't the first gems he and Angela Lark stole and hid in ice?"

"This is horrible," Maddie murmured.

Mike patted her back.

"I mean, he was a bit of a creep at times, but I never thought he was someone who could have a long list of offenses against him. I never even thought he was dangerous, just socially inept." She shivered and shrank deeper in her blanket.

"Same," Mike said grimly.

"It's one place the factory sells to, though," Carson pointed out. "A perfect cover. All Jayne would need was to receive the ice delivery at the station and then smuggle it out when nobody could see. Your average person isn't going to be suspicious of a man carrying a cooler."

"So, he sold the diamonds, but something went wrong." Maddie stroked her chin, a wicked gleam coming to her eye. "Maybe—"

Carson held up a hand. "I'm exhausted, and that storm out there is only getting worse. I don't mind if you two have a 'what if' session, but can it wait until we have decided what to do about this?"

Maddie flushed but nodded. "Given everything we know, Angela has to be the killer. I would never have thought it... but then I didn't think Mr. Hodgens was dangerous, either. I should get my internal radar checked."

"Don't feel bad about it, Maddie," Carson told her. He felt far older than forty-five today. Perhaps he was getting older and more jaded, and that weight was getting heavier every year. "I would rather you look for the best in people than see criminals everywhere."

"I can't be naïve, though. What if I assumed Angela was a good person and let something slip while investigating her?"

Carson shook his head. "You're too smart for that. It's why I always choose you for undercover."

"Hey," Mike said, stiffening. "What are you saying?"

"That you're theatrical and grandiose, which is great for our brainstorms," Carson said quickly, not wanting to offend him. "But you must admit that unless you're writing about a spy or hard-boiled detective, you often show your hand too much in these assignments."

Mike shrugged. "Okay. Yeah, I guess that's true."

"Are you going to arrest Angela, then?" Maddie asked.

"Right now, I don't have enough evidence. I just need the proof that she's the one that killed him."

Mike cleared his throat as he leaned forward, his palms flat on the table. "I don't think you'll find any such evidence."

Carson rubbed the back of his neck, frowning. "Why not?"

"I don't think she killed him."

"Then who?" Maddie asked, leaning forward.

Mike grinned, pleased to have a captive audience. "First, let me set the stage for what I believe happened."

Carson sighed. "Must you have the theatrics?"

"You said they were good for our brainstorming sessions."

That was true. Carson reluctantly nodded. He didn't have anyone at home to go to. And since Maddie suggested the two stay here tonight, he had every plan to accept that offer. He just wanted to move away from the case so they could have something lighter before bedtime.

"Willie Jayne. Career criminal, jewel thief, and always on the wrong side of the law. He gets himself a position at a gas station. Why? Perhaps he wanted to go straight. Perhaps the location meant he was central to distributing illicit drugs."

Carson nodded. It was what he had thought, too.

Mike sipped his wine again. "Maybe not, though. After his most recent stint in jail, maybe he couldn't find a job that would hire him— at least not on the books. Maybe a friend put him into a job at an ice factory. The job was hard, but he'd get paid under the table."

"Right. And then, at the factory, he notices the owner lives far beyond her means. Is she involved in something illegal or swimming in debt?" Maddie added.

"Exactly. He spies around a little, and a brilliant idea comes to him. All these blocks of ice are going out every day. Workers who were too old to care or were being paid under the table were also afraid of mixing up with the law. Perfect place to run illegal schemes."

Maddie nodded eagerly.

Carson grunted, not wanting to admit that the picture being painted seemed quite realistic. "So either he approached Angela or found evidence of her illegal activities. One way or another, he convinced her she has the perfect setup to smuggle diamonds."

"Exactly. As for what went wrong this time? Maybe one of them got greedy. They fought. One diamond got lost in the fight, and Angela locked Willie in the freezer. Now she doesn't know what to do with him. A dangerous man like that will kill her when he gets out."

"So she kills him," Carson supplied.

Mike shook his head. "I don't think she killed him, remember?"

"Then what?" Carson and Maddie asked in unison.

All Mike did was grin.

CHAPTER
SIX

MADDIE TAPPED her fingers on Carson's desk. Every few seconds, she glanced out into the bullpen, waiting for any sign of the detective returning. He'd been interrogating Angela Lark for almost three hours now, and she was getting antsy.

"What I still can't figure out is where the diamonds have gone," Maddie said, trying to distract herself.

"Me, either. I was up all night thinking, and I'm empty," Mike said.

He wrinkled his nose as he sipped the coffee he'd poured himself out of the police coffee pot. Maddie knew the signs and stuck her finger in his face to cut it off before it started.

"If you complain, you're walking home," she threatened.

Mike wrinkled his nose even more but straightened as the door opened. He set the coffee aside. Madeleine's heart jumped to her throat as Carson walked in. She quickly twined her hands together, holding her breath. She wanted to burst out with a million questions but kept them in.

Carson took a maddeningly long time to close the door before he turned to them. "It's just as you thought, Mike."

Maddie let out a whoosh of breath. The tension she'd been holding in suddenly released. Her shoulders slumped as she sat on the edge of the desk. "She and Willie Jayne have been using the factory to smuggle stuff in the ice since he took ownership of that gas station?"

"Yes. It's been small things gradually getting bigger. But she was still running herself into debt. The IRS came snooping around the factory, and she cut everything and ran. But she needed cash."

Carson sank into his chair, groaning.

Maddie could hardly contain her excitement. "And?"

"And so they hatched the plan to steal the diamonds. It was the most daring heist they pulled off, and everything went smoothly— until it didn't." Carson pulled a bottle of water from his desk drawer and drank it greedily.

Mike nodded as he leaned in. "And what happened? Was it Jayne or Angela who got greedy?"

"Both. Angela pocketed a handful of the diamonds before they went to freeze, and Jayne noticed they were missing. He took the block of ice and hid it somewhere. He was supposed to be her middleman, but when he confronted her about her ripping him off, it turned into a major fight. She lost one of the diamonds in the fight."

Mike shook his head. "So, he didn't even know she still had the diamonds on her."

"It probably saved her life," Carson agreed.

Maddie could envision it. The older woman facing off against, the taller, stronger man. "Does she have bruises?"

"Bad ones on her arms, torso, and back." Carson shook his head as he set the water bottle down.

Mike whistled. "He must have done a real number on her."

"He did. She tripped him and locked him in the freezer. She would let him out as soon as he told her where the diamonds were."

"But he didn't," Maddie said. "And fearing for her life, she turned the temperatures down and—"

Carson chuckled, holding up a hand. "Whoa, there. That isn't what happened."

Maddie frowned. "Then what did?"

"She came back to the freezer with the diamonds she took, thinking that would appease him; after everything that happened, she was afraid that doing anything else would lead to him killing her. But when she got there, she saw someone had turned the temperature below freezing."

Mike rubbed his eyes. "One of the other workers?"

"Oh, my," Maddie winced. "They couldn't know a person was in there."

Carson took another moment to bring in their expressions before he continued, "She panicked and opened the freezer, but he was dead."

"That still has to be manslaughter or something," Maddie argued.

Carson shook his head again. "He died of a heart attack. They found a massive rip in his aorta. The coroner says damage like that would have killed him in less than two minutes. He wouldn't have survived if he wasn't in the freezer."

"My goodness," Maddie pressed both hands to her chest. "So, he was dead before the temperature dropped?"

"Exactly."

Mike clicked his tongue against the roof of his mouth. "But then, where are the diamonds? Maddie and I were up all night and couldn't figure anything out. I'm loathed to say they're lost, but...."

He let it trail off, a pained expression on his face.

Maddie knew how he felt. One of the major reasons Carson got the two of them involved was that they didn't want the diamonds to slip out of their hands. Now, were they about to be forced to admit that this was beyond them?

"I just hate thinking that those diamonds are lost forever," Mike sighed as he slumped against the wall. "It just seems like a letdown for it to end this way."

"I know what you mean. But if nothing else, at least we have stopped Angela's smuggling ring," Carson said grimly.

"I suppose," Mike said, sounding unsatisfied.

Maddie raked her hand through her long hair. None of them wanted to admit that it wasn't good enough. She knew that not all questions had answers, but this? There had to be something! Giving up wasn't her style—nor was it Mike's or Carson's.

"Let's see if we can think of this another way," she blurted.

Carson gave her a puzzled look.

"He wouldn't take them to the station. Angela would look for them there. So, he couldn't have hidden them in his usual spots."

Mike nodded, looking a bit more energized. "That's right! It must be somewhere Willie had access to, but also somewhere Angela wouldn't think of looking."

"And somewhere he could send them without raising eyebrows," Carson added.

A slow smile grew over Madeline's face. Oh, yes. "I know where they are."

Both the men turned flabbergasted expressions to her.

"When I was undercover in the factory, Angela told me she had an ice storage facility in Spokane. It didn't seem relevant at the time."

Carson nodded, leaning forward. "But we were thinking of where a thief would hide the diamonds from the cops, not from another thief."

"Exactly!"

"And as a client who picked up the ice regularly," Mike said, his expression growing more animated, "nobody in the factory would think twice about him taking ice from the facility. So, he takes the diamonds to another of Angela's facilities and hides it in plain sight— she thinks he's hidden them or sold them out of her reach and so doesn't think to look."

Carson stood and grabbed his keys. "Looks to me like we have a trip to take."

"Maybe we'll come back with some ice in our pockets," Mike quipped.

Maddie groaned at the pun. "This is going to be a long trip, isn't it?"

"Not if we listen to music on the way—Vanilla Ice, anyone?"

MIKE FOLDED HIS ARMS, leaning against the wall as he watched the streams of water run off the enormous block of ice. Somewhere in there were two pounds of diamonds, minus a handful. It had been precisely where Maddie had figured it would be, in that storage facility in Spokane.

Lab techs worked around the ice, carefully chiseling off sections under the glare of multiple heat lamps. They had already gotten a few of the diamonds out.

"Once again, it's paid off to involve you two," Carson said proudly, standing to one side of Mike. "All I have to do is write my report now, and this case will be closed. Feels good."

"For sure," Maddie agreed on Mike's other side.

Mike hummed, nodding as he did so. As he watched the lab techs work, his mind raced over all the possibilities of this scene. Instead of diamonds, they could thaw out a corpse. A recent murder victim? An ancient humanoid? Would they find something enlightening the scientific world or unleashing a deadly plague?

He shook his head slightly, pulling himself back to the moment. "There's only one thing left that I'd like to know."

"What?" Madeleine's brow furrowed.

"What's going to happen to Angela?"

Carson grinned. "Oh, I'm sure they'll put her 'on ice' for the next twenty-five years."

The End

A LITTLE FROSTY

PROLOGUE

WINTER HAD OFFICIALLY SET in over Coeur d'Alene, Idaho, with the slow build of snowfall. In the New Year, they had almost eight inches sitting on the ground. It was pretty incredible, mused the man as he stood at the top of a large hill.

This was one of the best places for children to go sledding during the day. The snow had been packed hard over the hill. Fortunately for the man, it had been snowing almost steadily over the last few days, giving a lovely fresh coating. He looked down at the body he had brought here and shook his head. It was a shame that everything had to end this way.

"Death," he said to the body, "is the only constant. Nothing else in the world can be as constant as it. People like to say 'death and taxes,' but if civilization were to fall, taxes would end. Death? No. It wouldn't. You could argue that life is a constant, but the dinosaurs would disagree."

He chuckled, although there really wasn't anything funny about the whole situation. A sort of nervousness ran through him as he pulled a spray bottle from his pocket and misted down the body.

At this time of night, nobody would come to this hill, not when it was so far out of town. But he still had to work quickly—no time for philosophical musings. Once the body was sufficiently damp, he started rolling it. The fresh snow clung to the body, the dampness melting the snow's top layers while simultaneously freezing.

With one last shove, the body rolled under its momentum, picking up more snow. By the time it reached a standstill at the bottom of the hill, it was nothing more than a fat cylinder of white.

Nodding in satisfaction, the man settled into a wide toboggan, aiming the nose of it so he would avoid the dead object. He chuckled as he moved his body back and forth, edging the toboggan into a full slide down the hill. The wind rushed in his ears, and he couldn't help but laugh loudly.

He slid past the body and put his hands out, digging into the snow to stop himself. He was still chuckling as he dragged the toboggan back and rolled the body onto it.

"I haven't gone sledding since I was a kid," he said to the body as he hauled it back up the hill. "Then again, I haven't made a snowman since I was a kid, either. But don't worry, Ned. I'll make something beautiful for you."

CHAPTER
ONE

MIKE FROWNED AT THE DOOR, propped slightly open, which led into his best friend's house. Maddie wasn't usually so careless about such things. He knocked on the doorframe and pushed the door open further.

"Miss Moreau, are you home?" he called into the apartment.

Maddie appeared around the corner that led to her kitchen, her brow furrowed. "Miss Moreau? What's that about?"

Mike was relieved to see her all right; all he did was shrug as he stepped inside. He unwound the scarf from around his neck and shut the door, relishing the warmth of Maddie's apartment. She always kept it warmer than what he thought was strictly necessary. But it was nice to wear shorts and a t-shirt all the same.

"Can't I call you Miss Moreau?" he teased. "It is your name."

Maddie faked a bow toward him. "By all means, Mr. Malison. Please, enter my humble abode."

Mike snorted. He hung up his coat and peeled off the sweater he'd worn to walk over. "Why did you have your door open?"

"Because I got a new lock. It locks automatically whenever the door gets shut, and I didn't want to be bothered to unlock it for you," Maddie shrugged as she headed back into the kitchen. "I figure we can get started on work over breakfast. This plot is giving me a hard time, and I want to get it done so I can do that art class."

"Is Carson joining us today?" Mike asked.

"No, he got called off to something else."

Perfect. Mike grinned as he shut the door. He usually enjoyed having the older man around. He was an excellent grounder when Mike and Maddie started too deep into their flights of fancy. Lately, however, the sheer number of cases that Detective Carson Luttrell brought to them impeded Mike and Maddie's day jobs.

Mike loved to solve mysteries. He loved to figure out the clues and put together a scenario of what happened. Unfortunately, Carson couldn't pay them for the work they did. He had tried to convince his police chief to hire the two as consultants but had been shot down immediately.

Maddie came from a wealthy family. She worked because she liked to stay busy and found great creative freedom in dreaming up the plots she wrote as a freelancer. Mike, on the other hand, relied on his ghostwriting income.

Oh, he wasn't hard up for money by a long shot. He had built himself quite a successful career and had enough savings so he could take on interesting projects. It was wise to keep an income coming in when he was able.

"Smells delicious," Mike said.

He went to the cupboards and began taking out the utensils as Maddie flipped French Toast on the stove. He inhaled deeply. While the scent of eggs and butter was both strong, there was something else he couldn't quite put his finger on.

Maddie covered the frying pan with a lid. "Don't look. I put in a secret ingredient. I want to see if you figure it out."

"Interesting," Mike grinned. They often did this, sneaking different ingredients into their food.

He set the table and prepared the coffee as Maddie finished cooking breakfast. She plated the food, put syrup and whipped cream on the toast, and brought it to the table. They sat down together, and Mike sniffed the meal again.

"Cinnamon?" he guessed.

"Yes, but that's not the secret."

"Hmmm." Mike studied his food. "I saw half a dozen snowmen in your front yard this morning. I don't recall seeing them yesterday."

"There's a snowman contest happening in the town. Several families were out there all day yesterday, fighting over who had the best claim to the snow." Maddie cut her toast elegantly as she shook her head, her chestnut-brown hair bouncing slightly. "I never understood what's so exciting about snowmen."

Mike chuckled. "That's because you never got snow where you grew up."

"Vancouver gets some snow," Maddie protested. "Just... not much. So the city isn't ever prepared for it, despite winter happening every year. So many times when there was nothing but a skiff of snow on the ground and everything shut down."

"Ah, but that's because you so rarely got snow. Why bother with winter tires if you don't have a winter?" Mike chewed his food thoughtfully, trying to figure out what he was tasting. "Nutmeg?"

Maddie grinned. "No."

He took another taste. Something was different; he knew that. But what? "In any case, I feel bad for you, Maddie. Building snowmen was the highlight of my childhood."

"The highlight, eh?"

Mike grinned. "Maybe it's because I grew up on a farm, and we had lots of space to build them. It was always a family affair. When the holidays rolled around, my cousins would always visit, and we would build the best snowmen you can imagine."

"Perfectly round, sparkling white, 'with a corncob pipe, a button nose, and two eyes made of coal?' Did you also have a magic top hat that brought him to life?" Maddie teased, quoting the words of 'Frosty the Snowman.'

"Frosty had nothing on our snowmen."

Maddie rolled her eyes, though she was still smiling. She sipped her coffee. "Do tell."

"One year, we all worked together on a single snowman. We used the tractor to lift the body and head because they were heavy." Mike smiled as he remembered those childhood days. "My dad carved a giant piece of wood and painted it to look like a carrot, and we tied all our old scarves together to get around its neck."

"Impressive."

Mike sat back, idly eating as the childhood memories swept through him. Perhaps his new pet project should collect snowman memories from his cousins and compile a book to gift them next Christmas.

"Another year," he continued, "we built a snowman around our playhouse. It kept everything cozy and warm inside, and we thought it was perfectly camouflaged from the outside."

Maddie propped her elbow on the table and rested her chin in her hand. "So, was the highlight really the snowmen or the memories you share with your cousins?"

"The snowmen are the symbols for the memories," Mike replied. "I'm sure I have some pictures of them somewhere. I'll bring them over tomorrow."

"That sounds delightful." Maddie's expression took on a wistful look.

"What's wrong?"

"I'm not sure," Maddie said slowly. "Ever since I went home to Vancouver over the holidays, I've been melancholy. Coeur d'Alene is such a beautiful little town. I love it here. But I miss Canada. I miss my family. I miss the ocean."

Mike took her hand in his and squeezed lightly. "Perhaps you're feeling unfulfilled in life?"

"Perhaps. My younger sister announced that she was pregnant. Twenty-six years old, married, with a child on the way. There was a time when I thought I would have that life. And here I am, thirty years old, without so much as a boyfriend," Maddie shook her head. "Not that I actually want that life. I thought I did when I was a teen, but thank goodness, I was exposed to other ideas. I don't like babies, as it turns out."

"No?" Mike's brow furrowed. Through the years he had known Maddie, he couldn't remember a time when they talked about dating, marriage, or children.

Maddie shook her head. "No. They stress me out too much. Oh, they're adorable, and I will be the best aunt I can. But if I ever decide to have children, I think I'll foster them or adopt."

"I see. But your younger sister achieving those goals you once wanted for yourself is making you doubt your place in life, now?" Mike pushed gently.

"I suppose it could be. Or perhaps it's just that I wish I could have the simple nostalgia of childhood," she shrugged. "Anyway, I'm sorry I interrupted your childhood memories to be so dreadfully woe-is-me." A smile blossomed across her face. "Do you have any other snowmen tales?"

Before Mike could reply, there was a knock on the door. They shared a startled glance before Maddie left to answer it. Moments later, she returned with Carson trailing after her. He had dark circles under his eyes and an overall haggard look.

"Sorry for interrupting," the detective said as he slumped into a car. "This missing person's case is taking a toll on me. We received another tip yesterday that has turned out to be nothing."

"Missing person?" Mike leaned forward. Though he knew he needed to work, his focus was instantly on this case's possibilities. "You mean Ned Vande, that TikToker who went missing last week?"

Carson nodded. Maddie was busy making a third cup of coffee, so Mike slid his plate of French toast to Carson. It looked like the detective needed it more than he did.

"I've seen stuff about that on the news. Is it true that you suspect his wife might be—" she turned around and cried out. "Don't eat that!"

Carson had just been about to put his first bite of French toast in his mouth. He dropped the fork, looking startled.

Maddie hurried over and took the plate away while giving Carson his coffee. "Sorry. But you're allergic."

"Oh!" Mike's eyes widened. He let out a laugh as he slapped his knee. "So that's the secret ingredient! You made it with soy eggs!"

CHAPTER
TWO

MADDIE SHOOK her head sadly as she got a new pan to cook Carson breakfast. He protested, telling her she didn't need to make any special effort for him, but she was feeling antsy today.

An extensive project was due; no matter how hard she pressed herself, her brain just didn't want to work. It was beyond frustrating. Maybe a break was just what she needed. This could be a symptom of winter, yes, but it could also be a creative burnout. Perhaps it would help if she took a page from Mike's book and took up a physical job for a while. It would give her a fresh experience, at the very least.

"Now," she said once she had finished Carson's favorite, bacon and avocado on rye toast, "is this missing person's case something you want help on, or are you looking for a distraction?"

Mike shot her a doe-eyed look. She rolled her eyes at him. That look meant he had already latched onto the idea of helping Carson with it and wasn't happy that she had suggested a different topic of conversation.

"I'm not sure," Carson hedged. He took a big bite of his toast and closed his eyes, humming in satisfaction.

"Ned Vande," Mike quickly said, taking advantage of Carson's silence. "He made himself famous on TikTok, right? He was that stay-at-home dad who built a brand around being a good father and partner. Right?"

Maddie returned to her food. She was disappointed that her 'surprise ingredient' had been blown the way it did, but the dish was still delicious. It was the first time she had served Mike a vegan meal—well, vegetarian; she supposed since she had used whipped cow's cream as a topping—that he hadn't guessed it straight off. She had planned to use it as a springboard to ask Mike his thoughts on her perhaps going into culinary school.

As much as she would love to have another mysterious case to help Detective Luttrell solve, she needed some life advice right now. She loved her life and work, but there was that little voice in the back of her mind saying she was stuck in a rut.

She pushed the voice away, concentrating on her two friends. "Wasn't there a huge controversy recently where it turned out he actually had a nanny taking care of the kids and was cheating on his wife?"

Carson nodded. "It's more than rumor. He used the income from his TikTok videos to hire the labor in the house and started an affair. With Vande being such a public figure, it quite opens up the possibilities. His wife claims he left with his affair partner, but there have been no charges on his credit cards, no sightings, and it's looking more and more like murder."

Right. Maddie reminded herself that it wasn't yet murder, only a missing person. She cut up a strawberry and dipped it in the cream before putting it in her mouth.

"The wife did it," Mike said.

"Too cliché," Maddie protested. She waved her fork at him. "The kids did it. They got sick of being put online and mistreated by their father and so ganged up together to do away with him."

Mike's eyes gleamed. "And the mom is covering for them?"

Maddie considered it. "No," she finally said. "She's not covering for them. She's a workaholic who's barely at home—"

"Cliché," Mike protested. "And makes it appear the mom being the breadwinner is why her husband cheated."

"True. But she's still not covering for them. She kicked her husband out of the house when she found out he was having an affair, and he went missing right after. She assumes he ran off with his affair partner. The truth of it, the kids did it, and the nanny knows."

Mike arched a brow at her. "The nanny? Why would she hide it?"

"Because she loves those kids and is terrified that if she steps forward, the police will think she did it. After all—"

"After all," Carson broke in, chuckling as he shook his head, "why bother with the facts when you can have a pleasant flight of fancy?"

Maddie stuck her tongue out at him. Sometimes she thought that Carson's interjections like this were exactly how a big brother would act with his younger siblings, making her want to act like his little sister.

"Fine, fine." Mike waved a hand. "Then tell us, Detective, what are the details of this case?"

"A week ago, news broke that Ned Vande was lying to all his followers. Instantly, his feeds were full of threats; most aren't serious and just people who are chronically online." Carson licked the bacon grease off his fingers, then wiped them on a napkin. "However, Vande disappeared that night."

Maddie nodded. "What does the wife say happened?"

"She states she left work early after seeing the news, to be there with her children. When she arrived, she found the children with a nanny and no sign of her husband. He was having an affair with a young woman named Jean Lune, but she claims not to have seen him for almost two weeks."

Mike gathered the empty plates. "And the nanny?"

"She says that when she arrived in the morning to look after the children, Vande left at once without telling her where he was going. He left his cell phone at home but took his wallet with him."

"So she is the last to see him alive," Maddie mentioned. She stood to clean up the dishes, but Mike waved his hand at her.

Mike set the dishes beside the sink. "I'm done my coffee, and you still have half a mug left. Let me wash these up while you relax, okay?"

Maddie sighed as she leaned back into her chair. "Very well. Back to Vande. The nanny was the last to see him alive. Has his car been found?"

"No. Unfortunately, that's about all we have. A traffic camera took a picture of him running a red light in Spokane later that night, but the image is so blurry we don't know if it was actually Vande driving. There's been no sign of the car after that, even though we have an APB out on it." Carson shook his head, looking tired again.

"Then he must have dumped it," Mike concluded.

"Or he's dead," Maddie pointed out. "Or perhaps he's hiding low in a friend's rural cabin, or he went to Canada."

"In any case," Carson said as he stood from the table. "I don't want you two wrapping yourselves up in this case. I have people working on it. While I appreciate your input, my captain is getting rather pointed with his comments about your participation in my cases. It's best if we take a break for a bit."

Maddie sighed and finished her coffee. "Very well. I will have to finish my work, then, instead of procrastinating. Though procrastinating is so very fun."

"We've all been working hard lately," Mike said. He took Maddie's empty cup and washed it out.

Maddie smiled. She loved to cook but hated the cleanup. Mike disliked the cooking but found it calming to wash up. Together, it made for quite the enjoyable partnership. They worked together well in many ways; it was why they often paired up for their freelance ghostwriting.

In her opinion, a great friendship was always the basis for a great partnership.

"How tired are you?" Mike asked as he turned back to the two of them.

"Tired enough not to feel like doing anything," Carson replied. "Not tired enough to sleep. I have work, though."

"You can blow work off," Mike wheedled.

Maddie wrinkled her nose. "I'm not tired at all. I want to do something and break from the daily grind of life. Let's go to Hawaii."

Carson chuckled. "I don't think that's possible for me at the time being."

"Nor I," Mike said, but he was grinning. "Let's go around town looking at the snowmen, shall we? I have new neighbors in the cul-de-sac, and I would love to confuse them as to what sort of relationships I have. What do the two of you say?"

"I say that I will have to leave you to your drama-stirring," Carson said with a laugh. "I only stopped in because I wanted to let you both know I'll be busy the next few days. I need to head into the office."

Mike opened his mouth as though to argue, but Maddie cut in. "And we would not want to jeopardize your job. After all, you are the best detective in the precinct."

She appreciated having Carson in her life, but there were still a few things she wanted to talk to Mike alone about before bringing them to Carson's attention. She gave him a pointed look.

Carson returned the look. He understood her well, and Maddie knew he was picking up on her energy. "No, I wouldn't want to jeopardize anything. You both take lots of pictures of the snowmen, though. We can have our own judging party for them tonight at my place."

"Thank you," Maddie said. "Give me fifteen minutes, and I'll be ready to head out, Mike."

Mike wiped the crumbs off the table into his palm. "All right. Just remember to bring your notebook. Who knows, we might see or think of something important."

CHAPTER
THREE

MADDIE BREATHED the clean-scented air deeply. As much as she despised being cold in any shape, way, or form, there was still something peaceful and beautiful about this time of year. Everything was blanketed in fresh snow, a blank slate to write omens of the future.

She smiled to herself. It was a line from a story she had written when she was in elementary school and remained one of her favorite things she had ever written.

"You want to talk about work or have a complete mental break?" Mike asked next to her.

Unlike her, with two knitted caps, a scarf, and puffy ski pants paired with a parka, Mike wore a simple overcoat. It was unbuttoned down, and his scarf was hanging loose around his neck. Maddie wanted to be jealous of him, but he had warned her she was wearing too much for the day's temperature, and he was right.

So, naturally, she couldn't admit that even to herself, not for winter weather.

"Nothing about work at all," Maddie said fervently. "The last thing I want is to feel guilty that I'm enjoying this sunlight instead of being cooped up in my office, staring at a blank screen while I beat myself up for not having thoughts in my head."

Mike looped an arm around her shoulders as he laughed. "Ah, *mon Cheri*—I mean, *ma Cherie*," he corrected himself.

Maddie smiled. It had only taken him years to figure out that *mon* was the masculine form and *ma* the feminine. His name might be French, but he didn't learn the language.

"*Ma Cherie*," Mike started again, "I vould not vant you to beat yourself up."

"Is that supposed to be a French accent? It sounds more German," Maddie teased.

Mike shrugged. "So, this case that Carson is stuck on. What do you think? Is the man dead or just in hiding?"

They rounded the corner into the cul-de-sac Mike lived in. Every house on the street, besides Mike's, had a snowman in the front yard. Some of them were pretty elaborate, too. Maddie enjoyed looking at them as she considered Mike's question.

"As much as I don't condone what he did, I hope he's alive."

"Oh?"

Maddie stopped and stared at him. "Did you think I'd hope he was dead?"

Mike shook his head, holding his bare hands to the sunny air. "No, no. That's not what I mean at all. I was just wondering why it was. If you have any reasons besides decent people rarely wish death on others."

"I'm thinking of his children. Even if he wasn't the best of fathers, he was their primary caretaker for many years. I can't imagine how hard it would be for that person to die suddenly."

"But given what we know of him, there's a possibility he was abusive."

Maddie started walking again. "The possibility, yes. And if that is the case, they will be better off without that abuse in their lives. All the same, if I were in their position, I would rather my father be removed from my life in ways other than death."

"I suppose."

"I don't want to talk about this anymore," Maddie said briskly. "Let's admire these snowmen. Even your new neighbors have gotten into the spirit... although their snowman-making skills leave something to be desired."

She observed the massive mound of snow in their yard. While everyone else had lovingly shaped theirs into these perfectly round balls set one on top of each other, these neighbors had what appeared to be a sausage of snow standing straight up. Some work had been done to give it shape, but not much. It was even leaning to one side, propped up by a stepladder.

"It looks rather ugly, doesn't it?" Mike mused. "Maybe they're going for a Frankenstein theme?"

As they drew closer, Maddie noted that the hat on top of the snowman looked like it had come out of a trash bin. The scarf around its neck was full of moth holes, and a pair of snow boots stuck awkwardly out on either side of the thing.

It was all such a strange-looking thing that she couldn't help but giggle at the sight. The house was beautiful, and she knew it hadn't sold for cheap—she had considered buying it herself and moving out of the apartment. The back had the most enormous yard in the cul-de-sac, with this beautiful pergola the previous neighbors always strung with lights throughout winter.

So why did a family who could afford to buy such a house not be able to afford decent-looking accessories for their snowman?

She giggled again but attempted to swallow it down. She didn't want her first interaction with this family to be rude. Perhaps the decorations had sentimental value?

Mike rapped sharply on the door once they were on the front step. Footsteps echoed inside the house, and soon a tall, balding man answered. He had large, pale eyes and a red nose. With his full beard and the red shirt he wore, Maddie could have mistaken him for Santa Claus.

"Hello," Mike said brightly, holding out his hand. "Mike Malison here. I live in the greenhouse across the street. This here is Maddie, my friend."

"Hello," Maddie said with a polite nod.

The Santa Claus man smiled, though it appeared somewhat strained. "Henry Silver. It's a really friendly neighborhood here. My wife, Christine, and I have hardly had time to unpack with everyone coming over to say hello."

Maddie thought he was trying to make a point with that, but since Mike had said he wanted to leave them wondering about his relationships, she smiled brightly. "Oh, I know how that is! When I moved into my apartment, there were so many visitors all the time. People kept coming by and bringing me casseroles or pies. Of course, I want to offer the same to you and your wife, but I need to know if you have any allergies, how many people are in the house, and all that."

Henry seemed intrigued at the mention of food. "No, no allergies. It's just Christine and me here. But you don't have to make anything."

"It's no trouble. I'll whip up my special pumpkin pie for you." Maddie smiled again. She had never made pumpkin pie, but how hard could it be?

This is much better than trying to work on writing, she thought.

"Really," Henry started, but Mike interrupted.

"I will have to have you two come over some time. Do you like brandy? I have this excellent bottle of brandy."

"Henry," a voice called from inside the house. "Who is it?"

Henry sighed as though he had just been caught with a hand in the cookie jar. "Neighbors, dear."

A flurry of footsteps answered, and within a few seconds, a short, round woman with grey hair pulled into a knot at the top of her head was squeezing past Henry. Her cherry cheeks glowed as she clapped her hands. "Oh, visitors! How lovely. Please, please, come in."

Henry looked rankled, and it occurred to Maddie that this was exactly why he had been so short with them earlier. She felt a little bad at playing the overly friendly neighbor, but on the other hand, she loved getting into a role.

"Thank you so much," she gushed as she entered the house.

Mike made a discontented noise and followed her in.

"My, what a lovely end table," Maddie said, admiring the dark wood.

Really, it was the only thing there was to admire. Oddly, a grey-haired couple like this should have a lifetime's worth of furniture and momentums to fill a house like this. But there weren't even pictures on the walls.

"Thank you," Christine said. She wiped imaginary dust off the top of it. "I'm sorry I can't offer you anywhere to sit so we can talk. The movers have been an absolute nightmare. They said they would have brought our stuff in from the old house by now but do you see anything?"

She spread her arms out and shook her head in disgust.

Maddie nodded sympathetically. "Isn't it just awful how service workers pretend to work these days? Why, when I moved a piano into my apartment, they said they would be there at noon on the dot. They didn't even call me, I called them the next day, and it was still a week before I got that piano."

Christine clucked her tongue as she folded her arms. "Here I thought this town would be better than Spokane. At least the neighbors are friendly. And there's this delightful snowman contest."

By this time, Henry had slunk off somewhere, probably the kitchen or office. It seemed he didn't like to have visitors like his wife did.

"Yes, this snowman contest is wonderful," Mike agreed. "I haven't taken the time to put mine out yet, but I'm hoping to do so soon here."

Christine turned to Maddie. "And what about you, dear? Are you participating, or are there some rules against it at your apartment building?"

"Oh, I don't make snowmen. I don't like being cold," Maddie said. "I love yours, though. He looks so unique."

Christine laughed. "Oh, that thing? We're not done it yet. Henry's got this big plan in his skull about what he wants to happen with it, but he needs more equipment before it's finished. I threw on that old scarf and hat to trick the neighbors."

Mike winked at her. "Is it a trick when you tell the neighbors what's what?"

"Perhaps."

Maddie laughed. "I think it's a good joke."

"Thank you, Dear. Now, Henry and I are going to throw a little backyard party tomorrow. We just love that pergola, and it will be perfect for a wintertime barbeque." Christine smiled at the both of them. "I would love for you two to come."

"We'll be there," Mike said before Maddie could make up an excuse why she couldn't.

"Excellent!" Christine beamed at them, and Maddie didn't have the heart to say she wouldn't attend.

Ah, well. Perhaps a winter barbeque would be nice—if they didn't all freeze to death, that was.

CHAPTER
FOUR

MIKE WOULD HAVE ENJOYED SPENDING the whole day wandering around the town and playing distinct characters. Once they escaped from the Silver's new house, however, Maddie suggested they return to her apartment to get work done. Given how much work the two of them had to do, Mike reluctantly agreed.

They worked quickly after that, though, and got several days' worth of work done in that single afternoon, completing the project. Mike decided they would celebrate by ordering Chinese food and bingeing *The Witcher* until they fell asleep. Maddie happily agreed.

"Sometime I want to try my hand at Chinese dishes," she said as she bundled up for the walk to his house. "Authentic stuff. Maybe I should learn Mandarin and Cantonese to tour China and learn from chefs there."

"No, don't do that," Mike protested at once. Maddie gave him a shocked look, and, knowing he had one chance to claw this back, he gave her an exaggeratedly sad face. "I'd *miss* you."

"You could come with me."

"Carson would miss us."

Maddie laughed as she shoved her feet into boots. "If you're worried about him, we should invite him to dinner. You've been obsessing over this Ned Vande case all day, anyway."

"I have not."

"Have too."

"Have not."

Maddie bumped Mike with her shoulder, giggling. "Oh, so we're being immature today, are we?"

"Can't be mature with a fried brain," Mike grinned back at her, but it was to cover up the sudden knot in his stomach.

Between what Maddie had said this morning and all the hints she had been dropping throughout the day, he was worried that she was getting ready to pull up stakes here. He'd gotten very comfortable with the rhythm of their work, their partnership with ghostwriting and self-publishing.

He wasn't sure how difficult it would become to continue if he didn't have her excitement to fall back on. And worse, if she moved away, Coeur D'Alene might end up drab and boring. He loved this place. He loved being on the edge of the giant lake and being so close to places like Spokane and far enough away that he didn't feel suffocated by the city.

But what he really liked was having such close friends. Yes, he'd stay a good friend to Carson, but it wouldn't be the same without Maddie around.

He cleared his throat, shaking off those thoughts. Maybe it would be best to have Carson join them tonight, after all. It meant Maddie would avoid talking about all this moving stuff, at least.

He sent Carson a text and got one in reply, agreeing to the plan.

"You ever get the feeling that he only tags along with these sorts of things because he's worried we'll end up hurting ourselves?" Maddie asked once they were headed out of the apartment.

"Huh? No, I think he enjoys hanging out with us. It gives him that parental feeling without feeling responsible," Mike shrugged.

"I suppose, yeah."

She was quiet as they walked to the cul-de-sac. Carson was already waiting for them in his police cruiser. Even though he was a detective, the department was having a hard time with vehicles, and for the time being, Carson had to use the white car with *Coeur D'Alene Police Department* written along the side.

Snow was falling at this time, and Maddie had buried herself deep in the layers of her snow gear. They entered Mike's house while greeting each other, and Maddie made straight for his electric fireplace and turned it on.

"I don't know why you accepted that invitation to go to the Silvers' winter barbeque," she complained to Mike while he put away his snow stuff. She was still fully wrapped up. "I'm going to freeze to death."

"What's this? A winter barbeque?" Carson asked, one of his brows arched.

"Yeah. We can talk about it as we wait for the food," Mike said.

He headed into the kitchen, grabbed the menu of his favorite Chinese place in town, and then selected an appropriate wine-like beverage from his fridge. Wine-like because he liked to tease Maddie with the cheapest stuff. She knew where he kept the superb wine.

She didn't even make a face today when he set the wine-drink on the table. Though that could be because she was so focused on holding her fingers against the heat blower in the electric fireplace.

"Should I order the usual, or does anyone want something new?" Mike asked, pulling out his phone.

"Usual is good for me," Carson said.

Maddie hummed. "I want something new. Let's add some of that steam-fish roe and maybe the chicken feet."

Mike shared a startled look with Carson. Those were both options that, in the past, she had been adamant about not trying. *I know it's because I grew up in the blandest part of Vancouver, but I don't think I could eat anything if I had to look at the feet of any animal.*

"Are you feeling okay?" Carson asked in concern.

Maddie turned, a puzzled look on her face. "What? I think we need to try something new."

"Are you sure about the chicken feet?" Mike asked cautiously.

"I've been thinking about getting into some cooking school or taking a job in a kitchen somewhere as a break. The creative well doesn't run dry, but sometimes I tire of pumping out the ideas," Maddie said with a shake of her head. She finally took off her winter clothes when she spied the bottle on the table. "Ugh. Really? I know you still have that bottle I bought for you last week."

Mike picked up the wine-drink and waved it in her face. "But what happened to trying something new?"

Maddie opened her mouth, looking like she was about to argue, but then laughed. It was the brightest, most real laugh she'd given all week. "You're right! I shouldn't be such a snob. Chicken feet and wine to drink it is!"

At least the mood had lightened. Mike quickly ordered their food and got the glasses and utensils they needed. Carson cleared his throat as they all settled down to wait for the delivery.

"Now that we have that figured out. What's this about a barbeque at the Silvers' house?" His expression was neutral. Mike knew what that meant. He was brooding over something he didn't want to worry Maddie and Mike about.

"We stopped over to see them," Mike said. "They just moved into the cul-de-sac. They said they were having a party tomorrow in the pergola, and I accepted their invitation."

Carson frowned as he leaned forward. "Make up a reason to break that invitation."

Startled, Mike glanced at Maddie. She looked just as surprised. Carson rarely acted like this.

"Why?" Mike asked.

Carson pulled his hands over his face as though he was struggling with himself. Eventually, he shook his head. "I suppose the only option is to tell you. I believe Ned Vande was murdered, and Henry and Christine Silver are both suspects."

Mike nearly laughed out loud. As it was, he made a strangled sort of snorting noise. How could those grey-haired people be killers? He had seen images of Ned Vande. He was a tall, muscular man who had played football for almost a decade before an injury took him out of the game. Even Henry wasn't burly enough to take on a man like that.

"But they look like Santa and Mrs. Claus," Maddie protested.

"I know but looks can be deceiving." Carson picked up the wine-drink bottle and poured them each a cup. His dark expression slowly lightened, and he was chuckling when he set the bottle back down and handed out the drinks.

Maddie, sitting curled up in her favorite chair, frowned at him. As usual, she wore an oversized knitted sweater. The neck was too large and slipped off her shoulder as she took her drink. "What's funny?"

"Just this morning, I told you I would not involve you in this case, and less than a day later, suddenly, I'm telling you everything."

"You haven't told us anything yet," Mike pointed out. He leaned back on the couch and crossed his legs. "So. How are the Silvers connected to Ned Vande, and how could Santa Claus have killed the TikTok star?"

Carson sipped his drink and winced. Mike wasn't sure if it was the case or the taste he was wincing at. He waited, feeling himself edging closer to the edge of his seat with each passing second.

"First, you know that Ned Vande wasn't just cheating and lying to his viewers about what he did," Carson finally said, just as Mike thought he was about to fly apart at the seams.

"Oh?" Maddie pushed, yet somehow sounded polite about it. She had such an elegant aura around her.

"He has been under investigation by the IRS for some time," Carson continued. "It looked as though he might get money under the table. As it turned out, they were right... Ned Vande bought his internet popularity. The vast majority of his first influx of followers were bot accounts, and with them, he gamed the algorithm to end up everywhere."

Mike had to admit he was actually impressed by that.

"How did he get that money?" Maddie asked. "From what I know, he got laid off from his job, and he and his wife were struggling for money. That's why he started the channel."

Carson shook his head. "Smuggling."

Maddie's eyes widened. "You mean like that diamond smuggling case we solved last year? Was he involved in that?"

"It seems he might be, but I don't have any evidence for it, which brings me to the Silvers. I've looked into them, and I found they have been charged a dozen times for involvement in smuggling. Gems, drugs, black market artifacts. They've been doing this for decades all across the country. But nothing has stuck."

Mike thought of the hallway table in the Silver's house. Was it some ancient, rare antique? It looked like something that you could buy at Walmart. "Not enough evidence?"

"You could say that." Carson's gaze darkened. "Seems they're good at getting rid of the evidence."

"Oh, no," Maddie breathed. "You mean… witnesses?"

"That's exactly what I mean," Carson said grimly.

Mike leaned back, a chill settling over them. They seemed to be such charming, grandparent-like people! It just went to show you couldn't trust your eyes in these matters. He sucked on his teeth as he considered the situation.

"And you think Ned Vande was one of these witnesses?" Maddie asked.

Carson's expression only grew more serious. "Yes."

CHAPTER
FIVE

THE THREE OF them sat in silence. It was undoubtedly a grim outlook for sure; a missing man, known criminals in their midst. He imagined it would be even more shocking for his two young companions. After all, he had been careful not to reveal too much earlier since it would cause problems with the Captain if they had to give the credit for another solved case to civilians.

Mike finally finished his drink and set the empty glass down. "So, Ned Vande was involved in the Silvers' smuggling organization, and with the IRS sniffing around, they ended him rather than take the chance he'd squeal?"

"That's what it looks like," Carson agreed.

A ring came at the doorbell, announcing their food. Mike headed over to answer it, and Carson poured himself another drink. This beverage tasted nothing like wine. It was far too sweet. So sweet, in fact, that he couldn't taste the alcohol. Which meant he would need to be very careful with it.

"Here we go," Mike said as he returned. He set the boxes on the coffee table and handed Carson and Maddie their chopsticks. He settled back on the couch and grabbed an empty plate to pick himself up. "All right. The Silvers moved in a month ago."

"A month and they still have nothing in their house except this cheap end table in their entrance hallway," Maddie said, picking out a fish-and-roe ball and a chicken foot.

Carson took a few chicken feet himself. He had always loved these dishes; they reminded him of his first girlfriend's house. Of course, the taste was never quite the same, but the memories were good. "Do you think they could hide anything on the table?"

"I wondered if it might be an antique," Mike said.

Maddie shook her head. "No way. They got that thing from a thrift shop for ten bucks; I guarantee it. However, I noticed some scratches where the legs connect to the table. If they've changed it, they might use it for smuggling."

"Which is the FBI's jurisdiction—not that they listen to anything us detectives have to say." Carson attempted to keep his expression smooth.

He couldn't say he was surprised that the agents he'd talked to had completely dismissed his concerns. After all, this was hardly a central hub for the crime. He grunted as he speared a piece of broccoli with his chopsticks.

Mike toyed with his food. "There's that snowman, too."

"Snowman?" Maddie and Carson both repeated.

The two glanced at each other. Mike did things like this from time to time, talking about things that didn't seem relevant at all but often would open up the case to what really happened. It didn't solve things all the time, but it did often enough that it earned him a bit of grace.

"The snowman on the Silvers' yard. I knew it was strange. I think I just figured out why." Mike grinned and shoveled food into his mouth.

"Don't do that," Maddie complained.

Mike moved his food into a cheek. "Do what?"

Carson answered. "Don't be dramatic. Just tell us what you figured out about that snowman."

"It's not normal, is it?" Mike said.

"Finish your mouthful, then talk," Maddie ordered, looking faintly nauseated. She nibbled on the chicken foot, and Carson wasn't sure if it was her preconceived notions of the meal or Mike's full mouth giving her that expression.

Mike obliged, and after he'd wiped his mouth with a napkin, he leaned forward. "The snowman that the Silvers have in their front yard. It looks more like they've rolled snow around something and packed in the open parts that tried to make an actual snowman."

"Christine said they were planning on fixing it up," Maddie said doubtfully. She shook her head and continued even as Mike grinned. "But if their house is so empty after a month, they can't plan to stick around, so why would they even care about the contest? I feel Christine was just talking about the things that seemed off to answer our unasked questions."

Carson didn't like the sound of that. "Before we get further, I would prefer the two of you stay in Maddie's apartment or stay at my place tonight. The Silvers will have seen the cruiser outside, and I don't want them to decide you two are a threat."

Mike waved a hand at him. "We'll figure that out later. Back to the snowman."

"The snowman," Maddie repeated, sounding a little sarcastic. "The all-important snowman."

"They put it up before the contest was announced." Mike paused and looked between Maddie and Carson for his dramatic effect.

Carson couldn't help but feel an exasperated fondness well over him. "When did they put it up?" he pressed.

"About a week ago."

Maddie straightened. "Wait! What are you saying? You think—"

"Ned Vande is in the snowman?" Mike nodded. "I do. Mrs. Fenning was complaining about it a week ago. She told me they woke her up at three in the morning with a truck pulling into the cul-de-sac, and Henry Silver rolled a big pillar of snow out of the back."

Carson lowered his plate. The thought of a man being stuck in that snowman was grisly, but the temperatures had been well below freezing for some time. With the added insulation of the snow, it was unlikely that a corpse would thaw out enough to attract predators.

"Why didn't you say anything before now?" he demanded.

"I had nothing to base it on."

Carson bit back a sigh. Of course not. Carson himself had only learned the Silvers were involved in illegal activity recently, and his Captain had told him not to let Mike and Maddie know about it this time. It seemed to be a safe enough option until he learned the two had been invited into their house!

Catching his eye, Mike shook his head. "Until now, I thought they were just a couple of retired folks who moved into town and were busy visiting family as they set up. I would never have pegged them for criminals, let alone murderers."

"And that's exactly how they keep getting away with it," Carson said grimly.

He pulled his cell phone from his pocket. The Captain would not be happy to have his dinner interrupted, but if they could solve a missing person's case and bring in two criminals that the FBI was after? It would be enough for him to overlook any annoyance at Carson.

"I have to report this," he said. "Before I investigate."

"It's out in the open; can't you just knock it over and see what falls out?" Maddie asked.

Carson shook his head. "It's on private property, and with how rich the Silvers are from all their illegal activity, they can hire a slick lawyer. I don't want them to get off free because of some technicality."

"What if one of us knocked it over, then?" Mike suggested.

"Out of the question." Carson sent a text to the Captain, explaining that he may have just cracked the case.

Mike began eating again, but it was Maddie who frowned. "Why not? We could drink, so we're actually drunk, and go around knocking over all the snowmen. Then the Silvers won't know that we did it on purpose."

"It's too dangerous," Carson insisted.

His phone dinged. The Captain had responded, telling him to wait until the next day. Carson had to roll his eyes. While he had great respect for the old Captain, things had been getting sloppy in the precinct of late.

He stood and walked to the next room before calling his Captain.

He was greeted with, "Luttrell, I told you this would wait until tomorrow."

"It can't," Carson replied, keeping his voice level and flat. "I believe that I have found Ned Vande, Sir. Get me a warrant, and I'll prove it. It will be a good boost for the precinct," he added.

He wasn't up on TikTok and other social media platforms, but apparently, a big fuss was happening over this disappearance. They had had protestors camped outside the building for a few days even, though only a few, and they left as soon as they were confronted.

There was still the narrative making its rounds that the police were ignoring the case because Ned had been a stay-at-home dad, in any case. Some people just didn't want to accept that was a false persona that he'd presented to them.

"Bah. It can wait—"

"And if I'm right about who killed them, we'll have one up on the FBI," he added.

The Captain was quiet for a moment, then, "What do you need?"

Carson grinned.

CHAPTER
SIX

MIKE PUT his plate of food on the coffee table. His sense of triumph at figuring out the case faded as he looked at Maddie. Everything she'd been talking about and hinting at returned to him in a rush.

"Maddie, can I ask you something personal?" he asked, feeling oddly nervous, which was strange. He could talk to Maddie and Carson about anything. They were the only two people in the world he was this comfortable with.

"Yes, you can use this in your next story," Maddie replied.

Mike managed a small smile. "That's not what I meant. I meant personal about you."

"Oh. Personal how?"

Mike hesitated. "You haven't been yourself lately, and all this talk about wanting to do new things... it's got me a little concerned. Are you happy?"

Maddie blinked at him, the freckles on her nose making a little constellation of stars as she scrunched it up, deep in thought. "Yes. I'm happy."

"But you also feel stuck?"

"I feel... like I should do more with my life. Maybe I'm feeling burnt out. Maybe I'm feeling like life is repetitive right now, and I want a break from the ordinary to start appreciating the ordinary again."

She nibbled on a piece of ginger beef. "Maybe I need to expand my horizons."

Mike held his breath, looking for the right words, but the question burst out of him in a rush before he could think things through. "Are you doing to move away?"

Maddie's hazel eyes widened. "Move away? No! I love it here. Snow and all. I'm not moving anywhere. I was thinking about something like revamping my resume and getting a job at a restaurant or a bakery or something."

Relief washed over him as he slumped back on his couch. Suddenly all the worries he'd been trying to avoid all day seemed so silly he could have laughed at himself. What a thing to fret over when it wasn't even on Maddie's mind!

"I think that's a great idea," he said. "You've always been clever at cooking and baking and switching things up sometimes is always good."

Maddie smiled back at him. "You will not discourage me? We've been doing so much work together lately...."

"Maddie, I will never discourage you from trying new angles in life," Mike assured her. "And you know what else? If you want to talk about anything, just let me know. I'm here for you. Whether that's jobs or romance or children. I'm here."

Maddie put her plate down and got to her feet. She rounded the table and pulled Mike into a tight hug. "Thank you. I am thinking about fostering, but not now. I will not make that sort of commitment unless it's because I want to help the kids out. Not because I want to feel better about myself."

Mike hugged her back. "Of course, *ma Cherie*."

He kissed the top of her head and broke the hug, smiling at her.

The moment was broken by the sound of an engine starting outside. Under normal circumstances, it wouldn't have caught Mike's attention at all. Something about it tonight made the hairs on his arms stand on end.

His dark eyes met Maddie's hazel-green ones, and they both rushed to the front door at the same time.

A giant moving van stood outside of the Silvers' house. Mike's heart jumped to his throat. No! They were going to move the body, and then the truth of what happened to Ned Vande would vanish forever. Whatever criminal activity they had gotten him twisted up in would continue. How long before they were stopped?

How many more bodies?

"Get Carson," he said, his voice tense.

Maddie turned on her heel and rushed away. Something big moved on the other back side of the moving van, and a little voice worried that he was being foolish. But in the face of everything he had learned within the last few hours, he knew he couldn't let them get away with this.

He was out of the door before thinking of the implications of stopping himself. His bare feet kicked through the snow as he drove across the yard, heading toward the moving van and the two people on the other side.

"Help!" he yelled the first thing that came to mind, the only reason he'd be dashing out without even putting on his shoes. "Call 9-1-1! He's going to kill her!"

The massive pillar of snow containing Ned Vande dropped as Henry and Christine cried out. A dolly fell in the other direction, falling onto Henry's foot. He started hopping on his other foot, letting out a stream of pained curses.

"What are you talking about?" Christine demanded, grabbing Mike's arm. "Who's killing who?"

"The cop," Mike yelled.

Henry waved a hand at him. "Be quiet! You'll wake the neighbors!"

Oh. What a good idea! Mike almost grinned. "HELP!" he yelled louder than ever. "SOMEONE PLEASE HELP!"

"Mike!" Carson's voice came from behind them. He turned to see the detective rushing across the road.

"It's him!" Mike shouted. Carson would understand; they'd worked together often enough for him to catch on. At least, Mike hoped he would as he hid behind Henry and Christine. He raised his voice even louder. "He tried to kill Maddie!"

Carson came up short as the older couple looked at him bewilderedly. His eyes flickered to Mike, but just as Mike guessed, he knew what role to play.

"Mike don't be silly," Carson said, lifting his hands in a placating gesture. "You don't know what you saw."

Mike backed away from the Silvers toward their fallen snowman. Warrant or no warrant, he couldn't let them get away! "I saw everything. I saw you... and her... stay away! Oh, someone, please help! He'll kill me too."

"I don't know what's going on here, but I demand you both leave at once," Henry snarled.

Mike couldn't understand how Maddie thought he looked like Santa Claus. He ignored the Silvers as he backed slowly up. His legs hit the snowman, and he took a deep breath, then nodded once at Carson.

"Mike, let's go back to your home and talk about this," Carson said, creeping forward.

"No! You'll kill me too!" Mike threw himself back, knocking into the snowman.

Henry shouted.

Christine yelled.

And the wail of sirens rose in the distance.

THE NEXT DAY, Mike, Maddie, and Carson met again at Maddie's apartment. Mike sneezed into his mug of hot cocoa as Carson brought a small bottle of cold medicine and put it on the table beside him.

"Running after two known murderers like that was foolish," he said.

"I didn't know that you already had people on the way," Mike protested. His feet were still cold from his 'adventure.' "All I knew was that they loaded that snowman up and would take him away, and we'd never learn the truth."

"We would have caught them," Carson said.

Maddie settled into her chair again, holding a cup of tea. "Perhaps.

But they had time to split before the other police showed up, and if they had gotten to the highway, it would have been difficult to catch them before they dumped the body. I think Mike was fearless."

"Perhaps," Carson admitted. A smile tugged at his lips.

Sipping his coco, Mike fixed Carson with a stare. "Well? Don't hold us in suspense. What happened with the Silvers? Was Ned Vande in that snowman?"

"He was," Carson said. He settled on the couch. "And you were right hallway table. The legs had been hollowed out and filled with emeralds. The Silvers have confessed to it all in exchange for a prison sentence they can serve together. They had Vande smuggle in gems for them, and he used the excuse of being a TikTok star to get to places most people wouldn't."

Mike nodded. They had already figured that part out.

"When they learned he was in trouble with the IRS, they realized it was only a matter of time before he squealed. They leaked the information about him lying to his fans and cheating on his wife," Carson continued. "And when enough time had passed for things to get worse for him, they offered him a place to hide out. Once he was there, they killed him."

"And then put him in that snowman," Maddie concluded.

Carson nodded.

Mike sneezed again. "At least it's over," he said. "Although I'm disappointed that we've had this heat wave. All the snowmen have melted before the contest."

"Which reminds me...." Maddie grabbed a bag beside her chair and handed it to him. "For you."

Mike set his coco aside and took the bag, puzzled. He opened it up and stared. He held a small white figure in his hand. It had the shape of a woman, painted in something that glittered slightly. It had a tiny felt hat glued to its head and an orange toothpick on its nose.

"And what is this?" he asked.

Maddie grinned. "It's no man. Like 'snowman.' It-sno-man."

"No," Carson groaned. "That was awful."

Mike grinned at her. A 'no man' to commemorate the winter. It was no snowman, but he had fresh memories with Carson and Maddie.

"Thank you," he said. "It's perfect."

The End

A BAD EGG

PROLOGUE

THE HANDSOMELY DRESSED man swirled his glass of brandy, lounging on a leather chair as he watched the surveillance footage. It had been a long day with far too many hiccups. Sometimes he wondered why he was in this business. Sure, the pay was good, but he had to deal with such tedious problems...

A man came onto the screen, caught by the hidden camera. The viewer lowered his glass, scowling as the face of Josh Cardston became clear. The man just wouldn't give up, would he? At first, he'd been annoying, but now he was becoming a dangerous nuisance.

Something would have to be done about the Assistant District Attorney. While some ambition was admirable, getting in the way was not. Vancouver was a big place, big enough for them all to exist peacefully if people, such as Cardston, would just stick to their own lanes. It appeared some people had no sense of boundaries, though.

The man set his brandy down and turned off his video feed. He stood and moved to the window. The penthouse was well above the rest of downtown Vancouver, and a sea of stars lit the darkness of the night. He loved this sight, looking down on the world. It made him feel like a god, standing above all the little people down there who could only dream of the power he held, like a sword poised over their necks. He could bring that sword down at any moment, and it appeared Josh Cardston needed to be reminded of that.

The bright red and blue lights of some cop car flashed in the streets below, a reminder of the dangers of going after the ADA like this. However, Cardston had proven himself too dangerous an opponent to let him run about unchecked. It would have to be done carefully, though, to avoid the entanglement of the other cops.

No matter. The man stretched his arms over his head, then pulled out his cell phone. He'd get his best people on the matter, and within a month, Cardston would no longer be an issue he had to deal with.

For now, though, he could use some company.

"Hello, Ms. Moreau. I was wondering if you had time to spare to catch up with an old friend?"

CHAPTER
ONE

MADELEINE MOREAU FROWNED at her cell phone as it rang again. She pushed her chestnut brown bangs from her eyes and declined the call. She turned the sound off her phone. Being home in Vancouver for the Easter holidays was a welcome return to her roots. But, goodness, she wished that Quinton Fresh would stop calling her.

Fresh lived up to his name. There had been a time when Maddie went giddy for his attention, but she wasn't a teenager anymore. From what she heard about Fresh these days, however, he had never matured past that stage of life.

Shaking her head, she opened her message thread to Michael Malison, her best friend and writing partner.

The contest is about to start, and I'm turning the sound off my phone.

She waited a moment, hoping that he'd respond but doubting that he would. Mike worked as a prolific ghostwriter who was always full of boundless ideas, and Maddie knew all too well how wrapped up he could get in his work. It was one reason they got along so well together.

She mainly worked as a professional plotter. Coming up with the plots others could use was something she adored; creating characters and dreaming of all the mischief they could do was her passion. Some she loved too much to sell, and those she kept for herself.

Though writer's block sometimes hit the best of them, even Mike had dry spells despite seeming perfect in every regard.

Right now, though, he was amidst a truly stunning adventure. Maddie was excited to read the final project. She itched to be at her computer herself but had promised her parents that she wouldn't spend the entire visit chained to the desk.

And so that was how she ended up at this Easter Egg decorating contest. Her parents were off socializing, and Maddie knew most of the surrounding people. After all, she had run in these circles growing up... and she wouldn't trust any of them as far as she could spit. Not that a lady would spit in this company. She could only imagine the scandal that would ensue if she did.

With a chuckle, Maddie headed for the table her parents had bought for the family. She was looking forward to this, even if she had forgotten how much she hated being stuck in high society. Even though she had recently felt sorry for herself because she hadn't accomplished her childhood dreams, she was more than happy with the life she had created for herself in Coeur D'Alene, Idaho.

"Why, is that the Moreau's oldest girl?" a voice called out, clearly trying to catch her attention.

"I believe so, Mother," another voice said.

Maddie had turned her head automatically before she recognized who it was. She instantly regretted it, as she could no longer pretend she hadn't heard them. Instead, she put on a false smile as Judy and Jacob Cardston approached.

Weirdly, father, mother, and son all have the same initials, Maddie thought. Judy, a woman with striking red hair and eyes as sharp as her tongue, stopped before her.

"My dear, don't you look well?" Judy purred. She was, as usual, decked out in pearls and gold.

The Cardston family was very proud of the father, Josh, as the Assistant District Attorney. Still, they were quite gaudy about flashing around their wealth accumulated by the son's deals in the oil business. Maddie would have felt sorry for them if they weren't such acerbic people. They wanted to be part of 'high society,' but they didn't have the respectability that allowed them anywhere but tagging along at the fringes.

Although, Maddie mused, *that's just one more thing I dislike about 'high society.'*

She put on her most friendly smile as she nodded once at Judy. "Thank you so much, Mrs. Cardston. I'm very pleased to see you here as well. Will Mr. Cardston be joining us?"

Judy waved her hand. "Joshie is just so busy with that big trial with the drug cartel—"

"Now, Mother," Jacob chuckled, glancing around nervously. "We don't want to bore everyone with details of that horrible business. Ms. Moreau, will you be in Vancouver long?"

"Just the weekend," Maddie replied.

Jacob sidled a little closer, grinning widely, making Maddie very uncomfortable. "Perhaps I can convince you to stick around for a little longer? After all, since you had a headache the other day when I called—"

"I'm afraid not," Maddie interrupted. "I'm not sure if you have heard, but I am working closely with a… well-known figure," she blurted. Playing undercover was her favorite part when she and Mike helped their friend Carson solve cases. Now was a perfect place to pull that out again. She glanced around furtively. "My client would not wish for me to delay."

She had found that hinting at something secret was enough to make many people change their tact. A few would insist on knowing, but she always had the excuse of not being able to disclose anything. As it was, being so close to secrets satisfied most individuals.

Jacob, however, didn't seem to be much deterred. "Surely, an exception can be made? You could tell him you have family affairs to attend to."

"I'm afraid—" she started but was cut off.

Jacob stepped forward, too close. He opened his mouth and—

Maddie sighed in relief when the master of ceremonies stepped up to the mike and called for attention. How did everyone around her seem to know she was still single? It constantly felt like she was deflecting unwanted attention.

At least this is a charity event; she thought as she took her seat at the table again. Her parents made their way back toward her.

She peeked at her cell phone one last time, hoping to have a message from Mike. Her heart jumped to her throat when she saw she did. She skimmed it.

Call me when you have free time—I have exciting news!

Maddie couldn't help but chuckle. What exciting news would this be? Mike could be a bit dramatic, but she loved spending time with him. Rarely was she ever bored with her friend in her life… something she was intensely grateful for.

"What is that smile for?" her mother, Katherine, teased, taking a seat beside her.

"Nothing," Maddie replied. She sat through the master of ceremonies' opening remarks, only truly paying attention once the rules were explained.

"All eggs are raw and must be emptied before the painting can begin," he declared, his voice booming to the corners of the lavishly decorated hall. "You have been provided with the tools needed to blow them out, but also know this—the eggs must not go to waste. Every bit must be eaten before you paint. If you wish, you may cook them first, but you will be docked points."

Maddie felt herself turn a little green at that. The thought of eating raw eggs never sat well with her.

Beside her, her mother clapped her hands. "All right, so once we have half a dozen eggs blown out, I'll start drinking them," she said, a gleeful look in her eyes. "I've been practicing."

"I just don't understand how you can do that," Maddie's father said, looking as green as Maddie felt.

Katherine grinned. "Oh, Henry! I do it with ease, of course!"

"You have five minutes," the speaker said, "and then we will begin!"

"Five minutes," Maddie groaned. "Here I hoped that we'd get started already. I've already sorted out our paints and other supplies and organized them for optimum usage."

Her parents gave each other sly grins. Katherine looped an arm through hers and pulled her to her feet. "Well, I suppose we have just enough time to introduce you to Ben Hiddlestone, then."

Ben Hiddlestone? That was a name Maddie didn't know, but it tickled a recognition in the back of her brain. Was it a family who had moved back to Vancouver after leaving? She had to admit; she was curious to find out who this man was.

She wasn't fond of her mother's obvious ploy, though. All the same, she knew when to be polite and put on a smile as they approached a nearby table.

"Mr. Hiddlestone," Katherine trilled. "I'd like you to meet my daughter, Maddie. She's a writer like yourself."

The man at the table looked up. Maddie's heart jumped to her throat; Ben Hiddlestone! Now she knew that name. He was the author of a prolific mystery series that had taken the world by storm. She hadn't read any of the books but had watched the recently produced TV series with Mike and Carson.

Ben had deep, clear eyes, a stunning shade of blue. He got to his feet and shook Maddie's hand. "Nice to meet you, Maddie."

"You as well," Maddie said, trying to keep her cool. "But please don't like my mother's introduction fool you. I have some modest success with my writings, but I do it mostly for myself."

"If you write, it makes you a writer," Ben replied swiftly, the crooked grin on his face making Maddie's heart race.

She couldn't help but laugh. "Yes, I agree with you on that point. So, Mr. Hiddlestone—"

"Ben, please," he said.

"Ben. How long are you in town?"

CHAPTER
TWO

BEFORE BEN COULD REPLY, the chime indicated the contest had begun. Maddie frowned, but when Ben took his seat, she was pleased to see that he was at the table next to her and her parents.

Katherine scooted closer to Henry, giving Maddie a clever sort of grin. Maddie almost rolled her eyes, but she was too grateful. Usually, her mother's meddling in her life was unwelcome, but Ben was an interesting sort, and Maddie found herself grateful.

Oh dear, she thought as she took her seat, *Mother will never let me down.*

Her father pricked a hole in the top and bottom of the eggs, leaving her mother to blow out the insides and gobble them up; Maddie cleaned the delicate shells and set them to dry.

"Are you fine conversing with the enemy?" Ben asked her, also cleaning the eggs for his table.

"Of course," Maddie teased. "I am always interested in a good enemy redemption story."

Ben grinned at her. "To answer your question, I've been in Vancouver for a good year now. I didn't intend to move here. I never thought I would enjoy living in a city, but this place grabbed a firm hold of my heart, and I simply can't leave."

Maddie carefully cleaned out the first eggshell she was given, ignoring the sounds of her mother slurping up the raw egg.

"It's certainly vibrant," she agreed. "So many people with unique experiences. So much culture and centers where you can learn and grow."

Ben nodded, setting aside his first egg. "I will say, though, one year isn't long enough to meet many interesting people."

Maddie kept her smile on her face, but it was only polite. She viewed Ben with a new, guarded look. The thing she hated most about the society and culture was the tendency to write off people as non-interesting simply because they weren't wealthy or hadn't had the training in the unspoken rules of said culture.

"What, in your opinion, makes a person interesting?" she asked. "I have never found Vancouver lacking in that respect."

Ben hummed. "Indeed, Vancouver is not the one that is lacking. You might not realize, but I'm painfully shy. People only become interesting once I build up the courage to speak with them. For instance, you're an interesting person, Maddie, because I have strung my words together without scattering my thoughts across the floor like beads off a broken necklace."

Maddie laughed.

Ben grimaced. "I'm talking too florid, aren't I?"

"Not at all," Maddie assured him. "In fact, you are quite charming. I will have to keep my guard up. Otherwise, you will distract me from my task, and my team will fall behind."

"Then I must be more charming to distract you," Ben replied with a grin.

Their attention was drawn to the Cardston table, where Judy had gotten to her feet, holding her stomach. Jacob was busy cleaning the eggs, apparently not noticing or not caring that his mother looked in distress.

Ben jumped to his feet. "Mrs. Cardston, are you all right?"

Judy plastered a smile over her face. "Yes, yes. I'm fine. I'm afraid I drank some milk this morning before I realized it had gone off. It seems it's catching up with me, combined with these raw eggs. If you'll excuse me."

She hurried toward the lady's toilet. Madeline winced as she followed Judy with her eyes. It certainly was never pleasant to be caught with such difficulties in public. She searched in her purse, thinking she might have something she could offer the older woman.

"So, Maddie," Ben said as he resumed work, "what sorts of things do you write?"

Maddie looked up. She had met other authors in the past who looked down on what she did for a living and hoped Ben wouldn't be one of them. But then, if he was going to think less of her for it, it was best to get it out in the open immediately so as not to waste her time.

"Whatever strikes my fancy, more or less," she replied. "What I write, I write for myself and then self-publish once it's to my standards. I do well, but where I mostly shine is the plotting. I freelance for other authors who are having a hard time."

"Plotting?"

Maddie nodded. Her parents were nearly through all the eggs now, leaving her needing to catch up with cleaning. "I get bored with writing, to be honest. I mostly enjoy creating characters and plots. Of course, I work based on my client's specifications, but that makes me the happiest."

Ben glanced at his own pile of eggshells building up. "I see. I couldn't do that myself. Plotting is the hardest part for me. I will spend months on an outline, agonizing over every little detail. I can't write without it, though."

"I know a few people like that. My partner, Mike, can pull a whole novel out of a single sentence without planning, but I don't understand how he can do it."

"Your partner?" Ben asked, seeming a little deflated.

At first, Maddie didn't quite understand why he would be disappointed to hear that. Then it occurred to her that he thought she was speaking of a romantic partner. Her cheeks turned pink as her eyes widened. Was she reading too much into this, or was Ben Hiddlestone interested in her?

"My business partner," she said, watching him closely.

His face brightened, and her cheeks grew hot as her blush deepened. He leaned forward, his job forgotten. "Business partner?"

"Yes, in a manner of speaking. Mike has also succeeded in self-publishing but enjoys ghostwriting for other authors. I will often create the plot, and he'll write it. I must admit, he's a much better writer than I am." Maddie smiled as she thought of her friend. She wished he could be here with her; he'd have so much to say to Ben.

"If he's so good, why does he write for other people rather than himself?" Ben asked with a furrow in his brow. "I couldn't possibly. I will not put in the work so that someone else can get the credit."

"It's what he enjoys," Madeline shrugged.

Ben returned to cleaning off the eggshells. "I suppose that's as good of a reason as anything. My goals in writing must differ from his or yours. There's nothing wrong with that, is there?"

"Certainly not. If we all had the same goals, the competition would drive us to extinction."

Ben chortled. "I have never heard it said that way."

By this time, Jacob Cardston had already finished blowing out the eggs. He set the raw eggs aside, looking peeved as he peered at the lady's washroom. He grunted and painted the shells.

Maddie remembered how she had been looking for something for Mrs. Cardston and turned to her parents. "Can you clean up the shells for a bit? I'm going to see if Mrs. Cardston would like an antacid or something."

"I'll come with you," Katherine said, pushing from the table. She turned to Henry. "Is that all right?"

"Certainly, certainly," Henry replied. The eggs were emptied at this point, and he moved to Maddie's seat to continue the cleaning.

As they headed for the lady's washroom, Katherine slipped her arm into Maddie's. "So? You and Mr. Hiddlestone seem to have had a lively conversation."

"It's an interesting conversation, at least," Maddie agreed. "Though all we have talked about so far is work."

"Start somewhere," Katherine said, squeezing her daughter's hand.

Maddie smiled briefly as she swiped her chestnut-brown hair out of her eyes. Ben Hiddlestone sure was an interesting person. His genre wasn't one of Maddie's favorites. But now that she had met the man, she thought it might be prudent to check one of his books out from the library. She might not be in town for long, but it was always a good idea to have connections.

However, this wasn't a conversation she wanted with her mother. Not that Katherine was overly meddlesome in most instances, but she had a rather strict idea of how a young woman should live her life… and being single at thirty years old wasn't exactly following that path.

When they entered the lady's washrooms, it was oddly quiet.

"Mrs. Cardston?" Maddie called.

"Judy?" Katherine said.

An odd sort of feeling crept over Maddie. No sound came from any of the stalls; each one shut as though someone might be inside. She tentatively pushed open the first door, finding it empty.

"Maddie," Katherine said a little nervously. "Don't you think—"

"Stay here, Mother," Maddie said. She moved to the next stall and pushed it open. Empty. So were the third and fourth stalls.

Katherine seemed to get even more agitated. "She probably went back to the competition, and we just missed her."

The fifth and last stall in the washroom was locked. Madeline knocked on the door. "Mrs. Cardston? Are you in there? I have some Pepto Bismol that you could take for your stomach."

No answer. Bracing herself, Maddie crouched and peered beneath the door. Her heart slammed into her ribs, and she covered her mouth with her hand, shooting straight up. She whirled, turning to face her mother. Katherine's face was pale.

"What is it?" she asked in a trembling voice.

Maddie lowered her hand and straightened her shoulders. "Call 9-1-1. We need the police here immediately—I think Judy Cardston might have been murdered."

CHAPTER
THREE

MIKE'S STOMACH dropped as he approached the community hall where the egg-decorating contest was to occur. Police cars and an ambulance sat near the entrance, all flashing lights. He glanced at Detective Carson Luttrell and hurried his steps.

Inside the hall, they found a group of well-dressed people talking to one another in low voices. Various police officers were in the room, getting their statements. Mike knew all too well how the procedure happened. As he searched the crowd for Maddie, Carson headed toward one of the few men wearing a business suit. Mike followed; though he wanted to find Maddie, he also didn't want to end up having to search for both.

"Detective," Carson greeted with a nod. "I'm Carson Luttrell, a detective with the Coeur D'Alene police department."

"Coeur D'Alene?" the strange detective looked Carson up and down before nodding. "Ah, yes. I read about you in the paper. You solved a few rather large cases of gem smuggling. I'm Luke Jameson. What can I do for you?"

There was a certain guardedness in the way the detective spoke. Mike closed down his automatic thoughts on why that would be— while indeed there were juicy options for the man's jaded response, it didn't matter at the moment.

"What's happened?" Carson asked.

"A woman was found dead in the toilets. My ME's preliminary investigation suggests she was poisoned. The victim was seen leaving the room with stomach pains shortly before she was found dead," Detective Jameson folded his arms.

Carson drew a hand through his curly, dark hair. "I recognize that I have no jurisdiction here in Canada. But if I can be of any assistance, please let me know."

"Thank you. I'm not sure what you can do, though... after all, as you said, you have no jurisdiction."

Mike bit the tip of his tongue to stop laughing. Was it professional jealousy? Was that why Detective Jameson was being so cagey?

"My friend Mike here and I are looking for another friend of ours, Maddie Moreau," Carson continued. "She said she was going to be here. Would you know where she is?"

The detective's frown deepened as he looked between Mike and Carson. "Yes... she's over there with her parents," he nodded to a table and chairs behind the police line. "She and her mother found the body."

Relief swept through Mike as he finally caught sight of Maddie's chestnut hair. He left the two detectives and hurried toward her. She had an arm around the older woman, which must be her mother, but she suddenly looked up as though she could sense Mike's approach.

Her eyes widened, and she hurried over toward him. As soon as they reached one another, Maddie threw her arms around him.

"What are you doing here?"

Mike hugged her back tightly. "Carson ended up having an international conference here in Vancouver, and I came along to surprise you. Are you all right?"

Maddie nodded slowly. She released him and stepped back, letting out a shuddering breath. "I think so. I will be, at least. As many times as I have seen dead bodies while working with Carson on his cases, I never thought I'd be the one to find the body of someone I knew. Judy was lively and sociable, and then...."

She shuddered. Mike put his arm around her again. "It's going to be okay."

"I… I know." Maddie managed a small smile and guided Mike back to where her parents were waiting. "Mike, I'd like to introduce you to my mother, Katherine, and my father, Henry."

"Pleased to meet you," Mike said. "I just wish it were under better circumstances."

"I saw you were talking with the detective," Henry said without so much as a hello.

Katherine turned big, watery eyes toward him. "What did he say?"

"Preliminary findings are that Mrs. Cardston was poisoned," Mike said carefully. He didn't want to share too much of what the two detectives talked about. He glanced around the room, noting the dozens of eggs lying about.

Maddie nodded. "I thought so. She showed the signs. I also smelled something nutty in the eggs she had been eating before the police collected them for evidence. I guess cyanide was somehow introduced to the eggs; she had been eating them before she suddenly went to the washroom, clutching her stomach."

"Do you have to talk about it?" Katherine moaned.

Maddie turned to her mother. "Yes, I do. Mike and I have worked with Carson—Detective Luttrell—for many years now. I can understand if you don't want to hear us discuss the case, given what happened… it's just easier if I try to put emotional distance between the victim and me."

Mike almost thought Katherine would cry, but she only nodded once; she and Henry excused themselves, leaving Maddie and Mike alone. A sudden loud cry from the doors made them both turn.

"Oh dear," Maddie murmured, putting a hand on her chest.

Two new men had joined Detective Jameson. Carson was nowhere to be seen, but these two men hugged each other. One of them seemed to be on the verge of falling over. Mike touched Maddie's hand and gave her a quizzical look.

"The older one, wearing the blue shirt, is Josh Cardston. Judy's husband," Maddie whispered, nodding towards the man slowly slumping toward the floor. "The older one is his son, Jacob."

"Jacob seems to take it well," Mike murmured.

A voice spoke behind them. "I've spent some time with the Cardston's these last few days and concluded that the son has had to raise his parents emotionally. This would just be another example—him needing to comfort his father while his grief is ignored."

Mike turned, and shock flooded him when he saw who it was. Despite the situation, all he could do was stare, tongue-tied. Over the last few days, he'd read not one but three of Ben Hiddlestone's books, unable to put them down—and here the author was in the flesh.

Luckily, he didn't need to think of anything witty to say. By this time, Carson had joined them.

"Luttrell," Ben said, his brows arching in surprise. "What an unexpected pleasure!"

"Hiddlestone!" Carson eagerly shook Ben's hand. "It's been too long. Last I heard, you were out in LA. What brings you to Canada?"

"Research for a new book," Ben replied without missing a beat.

Mike choked on his surprise and coughed.

"Easy," Carson said, patting his back.

Mike shook him off. "You never told me you know Ben Hiddlestone!"

"You never asked."

"Why would I?" Mike shot back. "Am I supposed to ask you if you're the son of a Transylvanian vampire? No, because it's not something a normal person thinks about!"

Carson laughed and patted Mike's shoulder. "Easy, there. Yes, I know Ben. We met a few years back while he was writing his first book. A first book I hear did very well," Carson added with a smile to Ben.

Ben grinned back. "You and I will have to get together to catch up, Luttrell."

"Of course."

Carson looked at his two younger friends, and his expression sobered slightly. "In the meantime, I should get Maddie and Mike to somewhere we can talk. Maddie, where are your parents? I rented a minivan; I have room for everyone."

They moved off, though Mike kept throwing glances over his shoulder. Ben Hiddlestone!

Katherine and Henry both thanked Carson for the offer of a ride but assured him they had their own transportation; they invited Mike and Carson to their home for the evening, to which Mike looked to Maddie. Her expression was neutral as she shook her head.

"Maybe tomorrow," she said. "For tonight, I'm certain that Mike and Carson want to get to their hotel. You did say something about a conference you were attending?"

"Tomorrow," Carson said.

"Then perhaps Mike and I will spend time while you're busy with that." She turned back to her parents, smiling now. "I'll just go with them to make sure they can find the hotel. I'll get a taxi back home. Okay?"

Looking at her, you'd hardly know that anything was amiss. Mike knew her too well to believe that, though. Her parents were fooled entirely or excellent actors themselves. They kissed her cheeks and told her to tell them if she'd be home after dark.

Maddie was quiet on the way to their vehicle, and Mike also fell silent. Carson talked about the conference he was attending to fill the space left by them. As he continued talking as though nothing had happened, Mike felt a suspicion entering his mind.

Once they were at the hotel, Maddie ordered some pasta. The hotel room Carson had been given for the conference had been no good, on the other side of town and would have meant a long drive every day. So, he and Mike had shared a room closer to the conference location and Maddie's home.

The room they'd ended up with had two queen-sized beds sitting snugly against a wall, an enormous TV screen, a mini fridge, and little else. It was not exactly the grandest of rooms, but it was comfortable enough for them.

"This isn't like a case in Coeur D'Alene," Carson said abruptly when the pasta arrived. "We are not to go getting involved. Allow the police here to do their jobs, all right? I don't want you getting involved in something that could put you in danger."

Mike rolled his eyes. "Yes, Dad. But really, how come you never told me about Ben Hiddlestone? And, for that matter, why was he at an egg decorating contest?"

Carson shook his head, rolling his eyes upward as though asking for strength.

Maddie giggled for the first time at that. "It was a charity event. He must have been there to support the charity."

"Ah." Mike let it drop because Carson seemed to want him to. But he couldn't help but think... was that all there was to the story? Or was there more that Carson wasn't saying?

CHAPTER
FOUR

DETECTIVE JAMESON LOOKED LESS pleased when he was welcomed into Maddie's family room. Well, it was her parent's family room, but the detective wasn't there for them. They weren't even home, having gone to an Easter celebration in another part of town. Even a murder couldn't stop their social lives.

Maddie and Mike were catching up on the conference notes that Carson had taken for them during the day when the detective arrived. He brought with him a copy of the ME's report.

"I hope you understand this is a courtesy because your parents have been so generous in supporting the Vancouver Police Department," the detective said severely, a glimmer in his eyes stating that he wasn't happy about this at all.

"Thank you, Detective. I appreciate this more than you know," Maddie said in response. She gave him one of her most winning smiles, imagining herself as the innocent main character in a story full of intrigue and mystery. "I hope it wasn't too much trouble."

The detective seemed a little mollified but didn't protest when Maddie, Mike, and Carson went through the file. After a moment of reading, Maddie looked up at Detective Jameson.

"There was cyanide found on the *outside* of all the eggs?" she asked incredulously.

"Yes," Jameson said. "We—"

Maddie's phone rang, interrupting him. She dug it from her pocket. "You've got to be kidding me! Ugh, this man will not leave me alone."

Mike held his hand out, and she handed it over to him. He frowned. "Who's Quinton Fresh?"

"He's a flat-out jerk that doesn't know how to take no for an answer," Maddie seethed, folding her arms. "We met when we were teens at a dance, and he likes to harass me whenever I come back to Vancouver."

"I think he's only looking for a booty call; he never contacts me unless I'm in town, and then it's all, 'Oh, how about you swing by my place for a movie.' No matter how many times I tell him to leave me alone."

Mike answered the phone, ignoring Maddie's hiss. As he snarled into the phone, he put on a deeper voice, "Leave the lady alone."

Then he hung up.

Maddie stared at him. She'd never known him to act so toughly before! He chuckled and handed the phone back; a flush rose in her cheeks. "With any luck, that will keep him off your back."

"For a little while, at least," Maddie said. She smiled at Mike, pleased; if she remembered Quinton Fresh's character correctly, he was only intimidated by other men.

She smiled at her friend before turning back to Detective Jameson. "Pardon my manners, Detective. You were saying about the poison?"

Jameson squinted at her suspiciously. "All the shells tested positive for cyanide. Apparently, Jacob Cardston was poking holes in the ends and handing them to his mother to blow out and eat; then, he would clean the shells. Trace amounts were found on his hands."

"But how could there be enough on the shells to kill her?" Maddie pressed. "Wouldn't she have smelled the cyanide? I could smell it on her."

"Egg shells are highly porous," Jameson replied.

At this, Mike nodded. "It's for exchanging oxygen; you can smother or drown an egg because of it."

Jameson turned his frown to Mike. "Yes, exactly. The concentration of cyanide found inside the eggs is at much higher concentrations than on the shells. Neither Jacob nor Judy have a genetic condition that impairs their sense of smell. Those who sat around them assumed they had almond-flavored coffee."

"I see. And then when Mrs. Cardston consumed the raw eggs...." Maddie shook her head. "She never stood a chance, poor woman."

"But it still begs the question, why would anyone want to kill her?" Mike asked.

Detective Jameson opened his mouth, but Carson spoke first. "Didn't I tell you two not to get involved in this case?"

Both Maddie and Mike ducked their heads.

"You'll have to forgive them, Detective," Carson said to Jameson. "Maddie and Mike here often step in to help me in Coeur D'Alene. In fact, they were vital in arresting those jewel-smuggling rings you mentioned when we first met."

Jameson hummed, rocking back on his heels. "I see. So, you have some experience working with the police in an unofficial capacity?"

Maddie leaned forward. Something in the way he spoke showed that there was more to the question than simple curiosity. She studied the detective as he and Carson viewed each other. It was as though they were having a silent conversation, and Maddie had to wonder how they were already so in tune with one another.

Is it a detective thing? Or do they know one another more than they're letting on?

Eventually, Carson nodded once as though he was consenting to something. Maddie glanced at Mike, seeing the same excitement in his eyes that was growing more in her.

"There is something else you might do for this case, Miss Moreau," Detective Jameson said. "You see, we have reason to believe that Judy Cardston was targeted by organized crime; Josh Cardston is the ADA and has been working nonstop to collect enough evidence to charge the ringleader."

Maddie perched on the edge of her seat, nodding. She felt that if she pushed too much, Jameson would change his mind about whatever he planned to ask of her.

"Quinton Fresh. We believe he has used his wealth and position to start a rather prolific crime organization. Josh is far too distraught to continue his investigation, especially since it could have easily been both his wife and son killed in this attack," Jameson continued. He adjusted his cuffs, looking a little reluctant.

Maddie's stomach plummeted. "Oh, dear. So, you're saying that you want me to get close to Quinton to get information from him?"

"In a manner of speaking, yes. There is a… undercover officer that has been tasked with the job. However, getting a meeting with Fresh has proven impossible." Jameson looked even more reluctant to continue. He glanced at Carson once more.

"Is there something between you two?" Mike asked suddenly.

Carson arched a brow as he turned to Mike. "What do you mean?"

"You keep looking at one another as though you've made a previous agreement. Is there really a conference in town?" he demanded, standing now.

"Why would you think there isn't?"

"Carson, it was your idea that we come to Vancouver in the first place. It was your idea to surprise Maddie. I thought nothing of it, but why would the police department in Coeur D'Alene send you to Vancouver? In a completely different country?" Mike folded his arms as he narrowed his eyes at their older friend. "Or is there another reason?"

Jameson chuckled.

Maddie looked between the two detectives, and a sense of betrayal washed through her. It passed soon enough, though, and she burst out laughing. What a great joke! "So, you brought us here to help the Vancouver police to solve a crime?"

Carson stood. "I'm sorry for the deception, Maddie, Mike. Detective Jameson and I have known each other for many years. He reached out to me after hearing about our success with those smugglers in the States. I agreed to help, provided the two of you stayed out of it."

"Why would you want us to stay out of it?" Maddie demanded. "Haven't we proven useful in your cases?"

"Major crime in a big city like this isn't like in Coeur D'Alene; it's tough, dangerous. More competition means more ruthless criminals. I didn't want the two of you... well, I think you both know what you can often do." Carson gave them both pointed looks that made Maddie feel like a rebellious teenager rather than the thirty-year-old she was.

She nodded meekly. Oh, she knew exactly what he was talking about. Though Carson was a dear friend and would often come to them to muse over a case, he was also something of a big brother figure. Maddie didn't have any older siblings, just one younger sister. She imagined Carson would be what a brother would be.

Detective Jameson watched the exchange with some amusement. "And what are they like?"

Mike waved a hand. "Oh, it's just that we tend to let our imaginations run away with us from time to time."

"Carson was probably afraid that once we found out everything, we would plot out the murder like a storybook." Maddie paused, and a wicked grin spread over her face. Just as her younger sister loved to torment her, she loved to tease Carson. "For instance, I could say that Quinton Fresh is secretly in love with Josh Cardston."

"Oh, that's good," Mike said. "And he built up a false narrative in his head, thinking that Cardston loved him too."

Maddie nodded. "But as the ADA cracks down on his case against the criminal mastermind—"

"The illusion is broken," Mike finished.

"He concludes it's the woman's fault," Maddie said, annoyance tinging her voice again. "After all, he's just the sort of misogynist that will do that."

Mike agreed. "So, he takes out the wife, certain that once she's out of the way, his illusion will return. And in the meantime, he pursues the young woman he has been obsessed with since childhood—"

"Please." Maddie held up her hand, grimacing. "That's far enough. It's all well and good doing this sort of conjecture when we don't know the players but talking about people whose faces I know is a different matter—especially when one is my own!"

Carson sighed loudly. "And this is exactly what I was afraid of. Now. If you're done making up stories?"

"We are," Mike said with a pleasant nod.

"Then I have a task for you, Miss Moreau," Jameson said, focusing on Maddie. "And I'm afraid it will have some risk associated with it."

Maddie nodded once. She was perfectly fine with taking some risks. "Give me the job. I'll do the best I can."

CHAPTER FIVE

MADDIE TWITCHED, nervous as she waited at a steakhouse on Carrall Street. It was a pricy restaurant, just the sort a man looking to impress a lady would make a reservation at. *Or,* Maddie mused *the other way around.*

Of course, neither she nor the man she was going to meet— Quinton Fresh—had chosen the location. No, it was decided on by none other than Detective Jameson. After all, this wasn't a date; it was a sting. Maddie wasn't entirely sure how she was supposed to help the police in this case.

Well, that wasn't entirely true, either. After all, she was supposed to get Quinton here. The undercover officer Jameson had mentioned they contacted her and used this opportunity to get close to Fresh. With any luck, that meant he would interrupt the situation before she had to actually converse with Fresh...

That seemed more dangerous than any other undercover mission she'd had before. Not that she thought Quinton would now pull out a gun and wave it in her face. Because she might just drop dead from sheer boredom.

She hoped that her undercover contact would get here soon, though. She needed to know what she had to do when Quinton arrived.

"Well, hello! Maddie, wasn't it?" Ben Hiddlestone slid into the chair next to her.

Maddie jumped. She flushed slightly as she took in the dark blue suit he wore. He looked extremely attractive, that was for sure. "Um, yes. Mr. Hiddlestone. I didn't expect you to be here."

She swallowed, glancing around. What would the undercover officer think if he showed up to find her already occupied?

"I like to check out the fine dining establishments from time to time," Ben replied, reaching across the table to touch her hand. "It's research for my new book—The Dove Dies at Dawn."

Maddie's breath caught. That was the code she'd been given to know the name of her undercover contact! She forced herself to breathe in, calming herself and smiled. She was good at this; playing a role was her favorite part of doing this sort of work.

She could do this without tipping Quinton off what was happening.

"What's this book about?" she asked, keeping her tone cool.

"It's a crime novel. I'm stuck on a certain spot, though. As a plotter, maybe you can help? My heroine is setting up the villain, trying to get him and the hero alone together somehow." Quinton rested his elbow on the table. "I'm just not sure how she will do it."

"I see," Maddie glanced over his shoulder; Quinton had arrived and was currently searching the restaurant. "The problem is, your hero and heroine don't have time to devise a plan, do they?"

Ben straightened. "Exactly. The tension is rising, and the hero wants to ensure his lady love is out of danger before anything happens to her."

He gave her a significant look. Maddie waved to Quinton, not to let him know where she was so much as to let Ben know he had arrived. She put on her angriest face as she turned to Ben. Quinton was heading their way at this time but was too far to hear them.

She ducked her head, making sure he couldn't read her lips— which she doubted he could, but it was better to be safe than sorry. "Your heroine is going to help your hero bond with the villain. Nothing better to talk about than an irrational woman, right?"

"I wouldn't—" Ben started.

But Maddie surged to her feet. "How dare you! You misogynistic brute! I'm so sick of men who think they can just waltz into my life and demand my attention. You're just like him!"

She threw her arm out to full length, pointing accusingly at Quinton. He stopped, his eyes widening as she picked up her glass of water. Ben yelped as she dumped it over his head, and Maddie threw her hair over her shoulder, grabbing a second glass. She turned to Quinton, who tensed.

Maddie drained the glass in one swallow and threw it to the floor, shattering it—she would have to come back and apologize to the staff and pay them a tip once this was over.

"Why is it that I invite one man here to finally get him off my back only to be accosted by another absolute—I can't even say it!" She grabbed her purse and tucked it under her arm. "Never call me again, Quinton Fresh. And as for you—" she snarled as she turned to Ben. "I hope you rot!"

Maddie stormed off, pushing past Quinton as she did. She was already at the door by the time the hostess and manager got onto the floor. As she threw her weight onto the door, popping it open, she heard Quinton in the back.

"Women. There's no knowing what's going to set them off, is there?"

She smiled as she hurried to the car, where Mike and Carson were waiting for her. She slid into the front seat and quickly buckled up.

"I think it worked," she said as Mike pulled out from the parking spot. "At least... I hope it has."

THE NEXT DAY, Maddie was taking a walk along the beach, enjoying the mild spring morning, when Ben Hiddlestone suddenly fell in step next to her. Maddie jumped but quickly relaxed. She gave him a puzzled smile.

Ever since the bizarre happenings of the previous night, she had been pondering over what role Ben Hiddlestone had in all of this. She remembered how Carson had known him that day when Judy died, but how did that end up with Ben being an undercover police officer?

"So… you are an author, right?" she finally asked, glancing at him.

Ben smiled. "I am. And I'm sorry to have taken you by surprise. People know of my connections to law enforcement, but only so because it helps to research my writing. If they knew exactly how connected I was, I'd never be able to get close to the people I need to get close to."

Maddie hummed. She and Mike had been up most of the night creating elaborate situations in which Ben's role played center stage. "And what sort of people do you need to get close to?"

"People like Quinton Fresh. As an author, I can get close to people who would never allow the police near them. It works especially well when the mark is a fan of my work," Ben grimaced. "But Quinton would never see me. He's too full of himself to be in the presence of anyone who might draw more eyes than him."

"You have that right," Maddie agreed fervently.

"So, I must thank you for your aid last night," Ben continued, turning his face to the pale sky. Gulls wheeled and sang while the rolls of waves crashed onto the sand. "And more than thanks, Maddie. I was able to get close enough to Fresh to clone his phone and bug his home. Nobody else has ever gotten close enough… we'll know soon if he ordered Judy Cardston's death."

Maddie sighed in relief. It was a great boon to know that. Poor Judy hadn't deserved what happened to her, no matter how tacky and arrogant she had been. "Do you think the police will arrest him soon?"

"I can't comment more on an open investigation, you know that," Ben teased. He bumped her lightly, grinning.

"Of course." Knowing he couldn't say it, though, didn't ease the burning curiosity in Maddie's gut. A chill wind picked up, and she stuffed her hands into her pockets to warm them. "Can you give me a hint?"

Ben chuckled. "Perhaps a little one… if the police find so much as a drop of cyanide in Fresh's apartment, the Assistant District Attorney will bring the might of the law down on him."

"And with good reason. I can't imagine what pain Mr. Cardston must be going through, having lost his wife like that."

"I'm certain something will turn up," Ben said bracingly.

Maddie nodded. Quinton had always struck her as the arrogant kind. Ever since they first met, he had thrown money around as though it should be enough to get anything he wanted. He'd always had his circle, people he knew would never betray him because he pay rolled their entire lives.

Some might say that money didn't buy loyalty, but Quinton Fresh certainly didn't hold to that belief.

"Cardston will get what he wants," Ben said, his voice firm. "Quinton may have temporarily won relief, but he doesn't know what he did. I've never seen a man so determined before. I can't help but believe that Quinton made a grave mistake."

"Even if they find the cyanide, they won't know how he tainted the eggs," Maddie said. "There has to be something else, something we are missing."

"What, though?"

Maddie shook her head. She had no idea how to answer that. What, indeed?

Her phone buzzed, and she dug it from her pocket; it was Mike.

"Get back quickly," Mike said as soon as she answered. "I have the answers!"

"What answers?" Maddie asked at once. Mike loved to be dramatic. And asking questions to which she already knew the answer was one way Maddie supported his dramatics.

Mike's voice was high with delight. "The case, Maddie! I have the answers to the case!"

CHAPTER
SIX

MIKE WAS PACING back and forth in the hotel room by the time Maddie and Ben arrived. His eyes lit up when he saw the famous author, though he attempted to keep calm. It wasn't often that he could show off in front of someone he had such admiration for.

"Mr. Hiddlestone, I'm glad you're here," he said, extending his hand.

"Ben, please. And I couldn't resist! Tell me, how did you break the case?"

Mike glanced at his phone. "We should wait for Carson and Detective Jameson; they will arrive here shortly. If I'm right—and let's face it, I'm only wrong about twenty percent of the time—we will have an arrest by the end of the day!"

Maddie sat down. "Very well. Let's wait."

"Aren't you going to ask?" Mike pushed.

"You said we should wait, and so, we should wait," Maddie replied, smiling sweetly at him.

Ben leaned against the wall, looking between them with a half-smile on his face. "Why does it feel like I'm witnessing a ritual?"

"Because you are," Maddie said swiftly. "We do this all time."

"I see."

Mike had to chuckle; he had to admit it was a little silly. But it was also great fun. "Please don't let it put you off our methods. We have, after all, managed to resolve some very serious cases."

Ben waved a hand. "No, no. Of course not. I'm actually finding it very interesting. I would never have guessed that you were a couple at first. But now that I see you interact more, it's quite obvious."

"A couple?" Maddie repeated.

"We're not a couple," Mike said. He glanced at Maddie, his brow furrowed. "Right? I mean, we do work together and often eat together."

Maddie's expression changed, a light pink color rising in her cheeks and over her freckled nose. "If we have to ask, it means we're not a couple."

"I suppose!" Mike laughed as he turned back to Ben. "There, you see? We're not a couple."

Ben looked bemused. "I don't see... but I suppose it's just one of those mysteries, eh?"

"I suppose," Maddie repeated.

The door opened, admitting the two detectives. Mike smiled to see Carson's usual expression, trying to be stern but secretly amused. Jameson just looked plain confused. Suddenly, Mike felt a little nervous. One new person was simple enough to absorb into their normal routine, but two?

"All right," Carson said as he sat on one bed next to Maddie. "So, what have you figured out?"

"The eggs didn't kill her," Mike declared. He picked up the ME's report, flipped it open to the toxicology report, handed it to Jameson, and then found the report on the eggs. "There was a higher concentration in the eggs than in her system. I've been researching all morning; if she ingested any of those eggs, she should have had a higher amount in her system."

Jameson frowned as he checked over Mike's notes. "I thought there was something wrong with this."

Mike nodded, puffing out his chest. "Knowing that, I phoned the ME and had them run tests on the victim's stomach contents. They found no cyanide in those eggs. So, I had them check her body more carefully, and they discovered a small needle mark between her toes."

"She had a head injury, but we assumed it was caused when she fell," Ben said.

"I believe that the killer planned to poison her with the eggs. But they realized they had a better chance when they saw her enter the toilets." Mike walked back and forth, explaining his thoughts. "They followed her in, clubbed her over her head, and took off her shoe to inject the cyanide directly into her system."

Maddie and Carson listened with strict attention.

Mike paused and turned to his audience with a flair. "Then they put the cyanide in the eggs and on the shells afterward, during the chaos."

"Who was the killer, though?" Maddie asked, sitting on the edge of the bed. "Why would they need to remove the woman's shoe, inject her with the poison, and then put it back on her? Then poison the eggs?"

"We know who it was, Quinton Fresh," Jameson protested.

Mike shook his head slyly. "Quinton Fresh wasn't at the contest. He paid someone to do it."

"Who?"

"Someone who spilled cyanide on his hands when he killed Judy and had to cover it up somehow. Someone who simply didn't know what he was doing because he never had to think for himself before."

"Oh, no," Maddie breathed. "You don't mean… her own son? I never even noticed if he left his table!"

"Something he was counting on. After all, nobody cared about Jacob Cardston. They only cared about his father. He doesn't even have his own bank account; he was living off his parents still."

Jameson was silent as he processed this information. "You're saying Jacob Cardston murdered his own mother?"

"That's what I'm saying," Mike replied grimly. "And he's not the smartest man. Otherwise, he would have planned the murder better."

"It fits," Ben said as he pushed from the wall. "I'm sure with the bug I planted in Quinton's apartment; we'll be able to get the evidence we need."

Mike nodded. "He'll have paid in cash; find the cash, and I'm sure Jacob Cardston will tell the truth."

IT TOOK LESS than a day for Detective Jameson to find the money Quinton Fresh gave Jacob Cardston. It was a severe blow to Josh to learn his own son had murdered his mother. He confessed quickly, even admitting that he was supposed to kill Josh instead of Judy. But Jacob thought Quinton would take the fall and killed his mother, who had always controlled him.

Maddie sat with her legs curled under her, wearing an oversized shirt as she listened to Detective Jameson explain it all. She shook her head sadly. "To think it was all over greed."

"It's tragic, but thanks to you and Ben working together, we finally found the evidence we need to put Quinton Fresh behind bars. And he thinks it was Jacob who planted those bugs." Jameson shook his head, a grin tugging at his lips. "It almost seems a shame we have to protect the lout. But letting Fresh kill him would be ethically wrong. He'll serve his own jail sentence."

"And that is all we can hope for," Mike agreed.

Maddie chewed her lip as she stared into her coffee mug. It was good to have yet another case closed, although it was undoubtedly a shock to her parents when she admitted what part in solving it she had played. She had told them about the cases in Coeur D'Alene, but as it turned out, they thought she was exaggerating.

The question remained in her mind, though… no matter how much she tried to push it aside, she couldn't stop wondering why Ben Hiddlestone had thought she and Mike were a couple.

Some mysteries aren't supposed to be solved, she told herself firmly as she stood.

"Thank you for letting us know, Detective. If there's anything else, we can help you with—"

"I'll contact Carson," the detective replied.

Maddie smiled and headed into the kitchen. She didn't feel much like finishing her coffee. Too much caffeine. Maybe some nice soothing tea…

Once in the kitchen, her phone dinged. She pulled it out, and her heart fluttered, seeing it was from Ben.

I'm heading to the aquarium. Would you and Mike like to join me?

Maddie grinned as she typed back. They had already been planning to visit the Vancouver Aquarium. *We'll meet you there.*

Isn't this great? She thought as she poured out her coffee. *Mike is going to be thrilled.*

Her smile only grew wider. Yes, she was looking forward to going home, but this had been a better Easter than she expected. Apparently, eggs and chocolate weren't the only things she found!

The End

TAKING THE FALL

PROLOGUE

MIKE SAT AT HIS TYPEWRITER. It was old-fashioned, and he liked how it felt to type on it. Oh, he was quicker with a computer. But with the spring storm thundering outside and a chill in the air as winter slowly faded away, he had turned off the power in his home and lit a few candles for the ambiance he sought.

He had had a dream about a spooky paranormal mystery that he wanted desperately to write about. Unfortunately, it was one of those rare times that his well of imagination was dry.

He leaned back in this chair, his fingers resting on the worn keys of his typewriter. What was preventing him from writing?

Maybe it was that his closest friend, Maddie Moreau, was currently out to dinner with the handsome, well-known author Ben Hiddlestone.

No, that couldn't be it. While Mike would have liked to have been there, he wasn't jealous and was glad that Maddie had found another friend she could spend time with. He got along well with Ben, too. He didn't come to Coeur D'Alene very often, and it had been Mike who turned down his dinner invitation.

He needed to get this book written.

"So what is stopping me?" he wondered aloud.

Mike had often found he was better at figuring out problems if he spoke aloud, even if he only talked to himself.

His neighbors thought he was a strange fellow. Mike honestly thought it was quite funny and enjoyed making them believe he was even weirder than he was.

"If I'm not feeling left out of Maddie and Ben's dinner, maybe I'm hungry?" He mentally probed how he was feeling. "No, that's not it. I should get some water, though."

Pushing himself from his table, he went to the kitchen and got himself water. As he drank it, he thought more about his predicament.

Sighing, he shook his head. "No, I know exactly what is preventing me from writing. It's the Harding case."

A young woman, Katelyn Harding, had recently gone missing. Her family was convinced that it was her husband, but there was no evidence that the police could find that Katelyn was even dead. Mike was sure she was and that the husband had killed her.

The whole town was aflutter with the rumors of it, but no evidence to put the husband behind bars had been uncovered. Mike knew it wasn't his responsibility... but he just wished he could figure this out.

Only once the killer was arrested could he write this novel.

CHAPTER
ONE

THE BITE of frost in the air was delicious. Mike breathed in the scent as he walked along the path near the long lake Coeur D'Alene was built next to. Fall was a delightful time of year, with the trees having changed color and dead leaves crunching underfoot. Best of all, Halloween was approaching.

Oh, it was still too early for the decorations to have been brought out. But black cats, ghosts, and skeletons would soon be abounding.

Mike loved Halloween.

He came to a bench that looked over the lake and eased himself into it. He had been walking for over an hour, simply enjoying the weather. The sun beamed overhead, bringing with it the promise of another hot day. Cold in the mornings, pleasant at noon, fading to cold again at night. It was almost like all four seasons wrapped up in one day.

His phone dinged, announcing a text message. He pulled the device from his pocket, checking it. He'd received a message from his friend Detective Carson Luttrell.

Dinner at my place tonight. Burgers and beer. You in?

Sure thing!

Mike had to smile. Usually, his tastes ran a little more sophisticated than burgers and beer, but occasionally, he indulged in his childhood's wonderful tastes. When he was a kid growing up on a farm in the middle of nowhere, they had little.

He was confident that his current tastes were more because he didn't have the resources to drink expensive wines and eat filet mignon back then. He loved the freedom to buy such costly things. It reminded him that he no longer had one foot in poverty.

The barking of a dog drew his attention, and he looked up. It was a golden retriever, tail wagging as it ran toward him.

"Copper!" a woman running behind the retriever yelled. "Copper!"

The retriever, Copper, skidded to a stop. Its tail continued to wag, but it looked between Mike and the woman as though confused about what to do. Mike couldn't help but chuckle.

"Copper, come here," the woman yelled.

The retriever turned and trotted back to the woman. She grabbed his leash and shook her head, murmuring to the dog before she looked up at Mike.

"I'm sorry," she called. "I promise he's friendly. He was looking to make a new friend."

Mike stood. "It's all right. I had a lot of retrievers when I was a kid. I know what they're like. Can I say hello?"

The woman smiled as she approached. "Sure thing. Copper here would love that."

Mike walked over and crouched, scratching behind the dog's ears. Copper leaned into his scratch, his tongue lolling out and tail wagging even faster.

"You're a good boy, aren't you?" Mike crooned.

"He is when he listens," the woman agreed. "I only got him a few weeks ago from a rescue, but he's trying his best to learn. My name is Beatrice. Beatrice Eden. But I prefer to be called Tricia. I know it's not exactly a common nickname with Beatrice, but—"

She suddenly went silent, blushing.

Mike laughed as he straightened. "I don't know that it makes much difference. You like to be called Tricia; I'll call you Tricia. I'm Michael Malison, but you can call me Mike."

"Please to meet you, Mike." Tricia held out her hand, and Mike shook it. "I haven't seen you around the park before. Are you new?"

"No. I've lived here for quite a few years, but I usually walk on the other side of the lake. Do you mind if I walk with you for a bit? I miss having a dog. Can't keep one myself, allergies." Mike's face twisted. Itchy eyes and a stuffed-up head were nothing to laugh about.

Tricia's eyes widened. "Oh! I'm sorry if I'd known—"

"No, no, nothing to apologize for," Mike said. "They're too bad to deal with daily but not bad enough to give up a chance to pet one when the opportunity presents itself. Believe me, I'm willing to deal with the symptoms in the open air."

"I was going to let him go for a swim. The day's getting warmer, and there won't be many of them left," Tricia said.

Mike looked around and picked up a stick. "Mind if I play some fetch?"

Copper pranced on the spot; his eyes locked on the stick.

Tricia laughed as she unhooked his leash. "Go ahead."

With a mighty throw, the stick spun through the air, landing on the grassy field some distance away. Copper waited until it landed before he bolted forward, rushing to the fallen stick. He picked it up and trotted back to Mike and Tricia. He gently laid it down at Tricia's feet.

She picked up the stick and threw it.

"There are hypoallergenic dogs, you know," she said, laughing as she watched her dog. "If you really wanted one."

"I know," Mike said. "I've spent time with them… allergic to them, too. It's a curse."

"Ugh, I'm so sorry," Tricia said sympathetically.

Copper stopped near a copse of bushes.

"Bring the stick back," Tricia called.

Copper sniffed at the bushes, then backed away, whining. He barked quietly at first but grew in frequency and pitch.

Tricia and Mike glanced at each other in alarm. Copper kept barking, and they both rushed forward. Tricia grabbed Copper's collar and hauled him back, quickly clipping the leash back. The dog pressed into her legs, whining, and shaking now.

"What is it?" Tricia asked with her eyes on the bush.

Mike bent, peering into the dense foliage. The bushes were right against the water's edge, the lake lapping at their roots. Something bright yellow caught his eye. Mike crept closer, tense and ready to jump aside if something like a fox or raccoon attacked him out of self-defense.

His heart dropped to his stomach when a hand appeared beneath the bushes. It was pale, white. Yellow nail polish glimmered in the morning light.

Mike had seen enough bodies to know that this one was dead from just the color. He straightened and turned back to Tricia. "Call 9-1-1 and tell them we've found a body."

"What?" Tricia gasped. "A body?"

"Yes. Please hurry." Mike pulled his phone from his pocket. Then, to make sure Tricia knew he wasn't also calling 9-1-1, he added, "I have a friend in the police department. I'll phone him so he can get out here ASAP."

Tricia, visibly shaking now, dialed the emergency number while Mike called Carson. The detective answered after a few rings.

"Yes, it has to be burgers and beers," Carson laughed.

It took Mike a moment to understand what he was talking about. Right, the dinner. He shook his head, sighing. "No, it's not about that. I'm at the beach, and I've found a body."

He walked around the bushes, bracing himself to see what he would find on the other side. His heart dropped as he saw a young woman dressed in a bright yellow dress, the sort you'd see on women in the 1950s.

"A body?" Carson's tone immediately turned serious and business-like. "Where?"

Mike told him his location, then described what he could see. A young woman with chocolate-brown hair was lying face down among the bushes, partly in the water. It lapped at her skirt, making the fabric flare like she was still breathing.

"Are you sure she's dead?" Carson asked.

By the sounds, Mike knew he was rushing around, getting ready to head out. "She's dead, Carson. No living person has that color. There's another person here calling 9-1-1."

"Good," Carson said. "I'll be there in ten minutes."

"Thanks." Mike hung up, breathing deeply.

His day had certainly just taken a turn.

Tricia was still on the phone, and Mike hesitated as he flipped to Maddie's number. She had been in the zone when he left her apartment, so intent on her writing that she had hardly noticed when he'd made her a fresh cup of coffee.

Did he really want to interrupt her for this?

Mike sighed as he sent a text instead, telling her to call him if she had a moment. If it were him, he would want Maddie and Carson to let him know, but he would also want to be left alone. This was better; it allowed Maddie to interrupt herself or choose to reply.

Carson was at the lake in ten minutes, and soon after, more police and various emergency responders were there. Carson took control of the scene, and Mike helped set up a barrier, then retreated to stand near Tricia, kneeling next to Copper with her face buried in his golden-red fur.

"Are you all right?" he asked her.

"Oh, I'm all right," Tricia sighed. "I just never thought I'd find a body. It must be that young woman who went missing last week. What was her name? Carla Fletcher? I knew she'd be found dead. I just… I hope it's not her."

Mike patted Tricia's shoulder, trying to be comforting. Everyone knew about Carla Fletcher's disappearance. Her husband had been on the news, begging her to come home. He kept claiming that she had run off.

The darker whispers had said something far worse had happened to her.

Carson headed over to them, his expression grave.

"Is it…" Mike asked, his tone worried.

Carson nodded once. "Carla Fletcher. The ME thinks she died around midnight. But there's more, Mike… can we talk privately?"

CHAPTER
TWO

"WHAT IS IT, CARSON?" Mike asked, glancing toward the bushes where the body was.

"First, are you all right?" Concern filled Carson's expression.

Mike took a moment to assess himself. He was shaken, for sure, but he had already compartmentalized these events. His concern had been more for Tricia than himself. He rubbed his itchy eyes and realized why Carson was so concerned. His eyes were streaming, red, and puffy.

"Allergies," Mike explained. "I'm allergic to the dog, but I've been ignoring that to ensure Tricia is all right."

Carson's shoulders slumped slightly. "You're all right, then?"

"Yes, I believe so. It's not exactly run of the mill, but I'm ready to answer your questions." Mike straightened himself, resisting the urge to rub his eyes again. He rolled back his shoulders, feeling the tension lingering in his body. "So, what do you need me to do?"

Carson eyed him for a moment longer before he nodded once as though satisfied with Mike's answer. "We found Kevin Fletcher's body this morning. He was bashed in the head by something long and thin, like a crowbar. The ME's initial examination of Carla Fletcher's body shows a similar end to her."

That couldn't be a coincidence. Husband and wife both killed in the same fashion? Did that indicate the husband wasn't guilty, as everyone —including Mike—had assumed?

On the other hand,... "When was Carla killed? Is it possible that they somehow killed each other?"

"No, no. Kevin's body was still warm when found; we received an early morning call about his murder in his home. It's impossible that Carla could have smashed him over the head with him still being able to dump her body before returning to his home."

"How long?" Mike took a deep breath, bracing himself. He hadn't seen enough of Carla's body to guess how long she'd been dead.

Carson shook his head. "At least a day."

"Isn't it possible, then, for Kevin to have received the blow to his head, kill Carla, dump her body, then return to his home and die from the previous blow?" Mike suggested.

"No."

Mike opened his mouth to ask how Carson could be so sure but shut it again. There was only one reason for that certainty without a complete autopsy. The damage to Kevin Fletcher's head had to be too great to allow him to have survived anything.

"All right," Mike finally said. "So, Carla Fletcher was killed at least a day ago, and Kevin Fletcher was killed this morning. This might be the work of a serial killer, then. Someone who targets young couples?"

Carson's expression grew even grimmer. "I believe we are. I haven't told you, but there is something even more unsettling."

"What is it?"

"Later," Carson murmured as Tricia approached, clutching her dog's leash. "I will tell you and Maddie at the same time."

Waiting wasn't exactly a strong suit of Mike's, but he understood the need to wait. Although thinking of Maddie now made him realize he hadn't contacted his writing partner. As Tricia talked to Carson, Mike took a few steps away.

We'll need to reschedule the plan for today, he wrote. *The body of Carla Fletcher has been found. Carson and I will be around later to discuss it.*

He thought about writing that he had been the one to find the body, but that would be better to discuss in person. The details about the yellow 50's dress, both Carla and Kevin being murdered in the same way, and this mysterious 'unsettling' information that Carson was loath to share was adding up to bring a shiver in Mike's spine.

A moment later, Maddie replied. *Let me know when you're on your way. I'll have coffee and food for you both.*

Mike smiled softly to himself. Coffee and food were the perfect thing to discuss the case over.

"I don't have any other questions for you at the moment," Carson told Tricia. "If you think of anything else I should know, you can call me at this number."

He handed over a business card, then glanced over at Mike. "And if it's something that you aren't certain is relevant, you can bring it up to Mike. He often works with me on my cases and will have a better idea of whether to share it with me."

A look almost like a smile played about Carson's lips. Tricia, for her part, flushed and looked pleased. She took her leave, and Mike walked with her to the end of the path.

"If you need to talk about what happened, let me know," Mike told her. He patted Copper's head. "And keep up the good work with this good boy."

"I will, on both counts," Tricia replied.

"Thank you."

Carson nodded to Mike to follow him, and the two went to Carson's car. Once they were heading for Maddie's apartment, Mike took the time to study his friend. The detective was a master at controlling his emotions and never losing his cool. Today he looked stressed, however.

It couldn't be good. The captain of Carson's precinct didn't like how Carson often had Mike and Maddie help him with his cases. Was that the cause of his stress today, or was it the case itself?

They arrived at Maddie's apartment. As soon as they stepped inside, the scent of fresh coffee and quiche met Mike's nostrils. His mouth watered; he had eaten nothing yet, and the smell of food reminded him of how hungry he was. He quickly went to the kitchen and pulled plates from the cupboard.

"I already set the table," Maddie said, shooing him off.

"Oh... you didn't have to go through the trouble," Mike started.

Maddie waved a hand. "The quiche was already in the oven, and it's not like making coffee and setting the table takes any time. Go sit down, and I'll finish up here."

Mike smiled at her. Her chocolate-brown hair was pulled back into a braid this morning. Her oversized sweatshirt slipped off one shoulder to reveal a second sweatshirt beneath it. It wasn't even that cold of a day today.

"Is that a fashion choice, or should I make you go to the doctor?" Mike asked, stepping aside for Maddie to work.

She frowned at him, silently questioning him.

"You're always so cold, and you're wearing two sweaters. Should I be worried about your health? There could be several reasons you'd be cold when it's not that cold."

Maddie gave him the indulgent, amused smile that always made his heart skip half a beat. "I'm not cold. I just wanted to coziness. Actually, I got too hot earlier and opened up the windows to make it colder in here."

Mike shook his head but smiled.

At Maddie's urging, he sat at the table. Maddie served up the quiche, coffee, and toast. Mike started eating eagerly, enjoying the savory taste on his tongue. He thought he was eating fast, but he was only half done when he looked up to find that Carson was serving himself a second piece.

"Have you been neglecting to feed yourself again?" Maddie asked severely.

"Only because I know you're such a superb cook," the detective replied with a smirk.

Maddie leaned her elbows on the table as she bit off a sizeable chunk of her toast. "Hmm. I'll be flattered enough to let you get away with that. Now, what's about this case?"

Carson ate again with gusto. Mike laid down his fork. He explained about finding Carla Fletcher's body and the added death of Kevin Fletcher the same morning. As she listened, Maddie's expression became grimmer and grimmer.

Once Mike was done, he picked up his coffee and took a big gulp.

Somehow recounting the events made him even more exhausted than he had been moments ago.

"And before we came here, Carson said he had even more unsettling information to give us," he finished, then sipped his coffee again. His dark eyes moved to the detective's face and remained unwavering on him.

Carson, by this time, had finished his second piece of quiche. He eyed the remainders with apparent hunger. But when he looked up between the two writers, his shoulders sagged.

"It's that bad, is it?" Maddie asked, her voice growing gentler.

"They aren't the only bodies found in the last forty-eight hours," Carson said. He gazed into his mug, a dark shadow crossing his face. "We found two others just two days ago."

Mike pressed his palms into the table. He hadn't even been aware that anyone else was missing. "Who? How have you kept it a secret?"

"The department has been cautious about this. We don't want to start a panic." Carson took a deep breath. "We believe that the first body we found was Katelyn Harding."

All the air seemed to disappear around Mike. His head spun. Katelyn had gone missing a year ago! How had she been found now? He opened his mouth, wanting to ask, but the words got caught in his throat.

Maddie asked the question that evaded Mike. "You said you found two other bodies."

Carson drained his coffee and pushed back from the table, looking even grimmer than before. "We believe the second body to be Edmund Harding, Katelyn's husband... also killed by a blow to the head."

CHAPTER
THREE

MADDIE STOOD FACING THE WINDOW; the autumn leaves blew this way and that. A strong wind had ripped several more leaves from the trees, which grew ever more naked. Fall always set a melancholy mood, giving her a languid sense of time. It wasn't precisely depressing, not exactly happy. It was more like a time to stop and think about the year.

Mike and Carson continued to discuss the case behind her. Her hands wrapped around her hot mug of coffee as she listened to them.

"It can't be a coincidence that two couples have been found so recently," Mike said. "How long ago were Katelyn and Edmund killed?"

"I'm still waiting on information about that," Carson replied.

Maddie turned from the window and returned to the table. Only one slice of the quiche was left, but by this time, it seemed her guests were full. She had eaten a small breakfast just before they arrived, so she was pretty full.

"You must have some idea, though," she said as she slid into the chair next to Mike.

Katelyn's disappearance a year ago had hit him very hard then, and she still wasn't entirely sure why. She could only guess that the discovery of her body would affect him now. She gave him a worried look, but he was too focused on Carson to realize it.

The detective hummed as he stretched his back. His eyes were drooping; between that and how he had scarfed down the food, Maddie was sure he wasn't taking care of himself. Of course, that was understandable, given that he was dealing with such a heavy case.

Carson glanced at her, then at Mike, the concern evident on his face.

With a sigh, Mike shook his head. "I know I was a little obsessed with trying to find Katelyn last year, but I'd worked through that. I will not start obsessing about it again... but you have to admit that the cases are similar enough that there's the possibility of a serial killer targeting young couples."

"It's possible," Carson agreed. He spread his hands. "From what it looked like, Katelyn had been killed last year. As for Edmund, he looked as though he'd been killed just a few weeks ago. They were found together, though. Edmund's body had been dumped on top of the place where Katelyn was buried, almost as though someone hoped we'd find her."

"And both were killed by a blow to the head?" Maddie pressed.

Carson nodded.

Maddie considered the situation for a moment, then nodded once to herself. No force on this planet would make her believe Mike was at all connected to these deaths, but she had to know exactly why he was so concerned about Katelyn.

"Let's go to the living room," she suggested. Everyone sitting at the dining table was feeling awkward.

Both men nodded. They moved to the living room, where Carson sat in the recliner and put his feet up. He looked so exhausted that Maddie had to retrieve a fuzzy blanket and tuck it around him. He might be fifteen years older than she and Mike and treat them like one would younger siblings, but sometimes Maddie had motherly urges that she couldn't help but indulge.

Usually, Carson would laugh at her fussing over him. It was a sign of his exhaustion that he took it without comment.

With him taken care of, Maddie sat on the couch and curled her legs under her, turning her focus to Mike. She rested her chin in her hand, considering how to ask the question bouncing around in her mind.

Mike seemed to understand what she needed to know without her asking. He sighed heavily. "I didn't know Katelyn or her husband. It's just that when she went missing, and I saw pictures of her, it reminded me of a missing persons' case from my childhood."

Carson hummed. "Tell us about it if it's not too difficult."

"Well, there isn't much to say... You both know I grew up on a farm. Our school was tiny. Rather than being divided between elementary, middle, and high school, it was all in one building. So I got to know all the teachers very well." Mike paused and straightened the cuffs of his sleeves.

"And... did something happen to one of them?" Maddie pressed.

Mike nodded, not looking at her. "Mrs. Crabtree. She was the kindergarten teacher, and everyone loved her. I liked volunteering in her room because she was so pretty and kind... I was a teenager," he added quickly, looking sheepish. "And though I'm sure my crush was obvious, Mrs. Crabtree ignored it. I felt safe around her."

Maddie smiled softly. She well understood the massive crushes she had on older men when she was a teen as well. Something was alluring about the maturity she was sure they possessed.

"Anyway, I noticed from time to time she had bruises she explained away as being clumsy. But she was the most graceful person I knew." Mike's shoulders were hunched as he let out a heavy breath. "When she went missing, everyone assumed she had run off from her husband."

"Oh," Maddie murmured. Her heart ached for Mike.

He ran a hand through his dark hair. "I knew she hadn't. The day before she went missing, she had promised to bring me some of her Shakespeare collection to borrow. And she left her favorite cardigan in the classroom. I can't tell you why such a simple thing made me so certain... but I knew her husband had killed her."

Carson spoke for the first time in a while. "You can't discount that gut feeling."

"I know that now. But in those days, the police wouldn't listen to me."

Maddie hurried over to Mike's side and put her arms around him. "Did they ever find her?"

Mike nodded slowly. "I did. The family had a golden retriever, and I stole her cardigan. The dog hadn't been trained to track a scent but by some miracle...."

He shrugged, his expression dark.

"And was her husband arrested?" Maddie asked.

"Yes. But it didn't bring her back."

"No wonder Katelyn's disappearance hit you so hard," Maddie rubbed his back. "It brought up that childhood trauma. Especially with so much of the husband's story being that she had just run off for no reason."

Mike nodded.

"Well, we found her now," Carson said. "And no, it doesn't bring her back, but her family will receive some closure. It's an awful thing. Edmund Harding was a terrible bully. When I investigated her disappearance, I heard the most awful things about him."

Surprise washed through Maddie as she looked up at him. "You investigated her case? And didn't tell us?"

Carson smiled wryly as he pushed back the chair, laying a little flatter. "I was strictly forbidden to by the captain. You know how he is."

Maddie wrinkled her nose. She knew that indeed. "Well, I suppose that's a good reason for you not to tell us, then."

"What did you hear?" Mike pushed.

"He was a bully," Carson said. "Not just to his wife, but to everyone. A neighbor had a dog that would bark a few times at night, so Edmund poisoned it. Another neighbor had a collection of gnomes Edmund didn't like, so he drove his truck through her garden beds and destroyed them all."

Maddie gaped. "Why wasn't he arrested for doing those things?"

"Because he had a friend on the force," Carson replied grimly. "A friend who would just make his troubles disappear. When I learned that, I was ready to commit a crime myself... I knew some of my colleagues were corrupt, but I didn't realize it went so... *deep*."

"Was it the captain?" Maddie asked, her eyes widening.

"No. I can't tell you who it is, though... he's still under investigation a year later." Carson shook his head. "But as I was saying. None of the children in the street would dare set foot in his yard since he went after them with a chainsaw one year during Halloween. And I'm not talking about teenagers, either. These were kids under ten."

Mike made a furious noise in his throat. "He seems like a monster! Why would anyone want to scare children like that?"

Maddie folded her arms as she moved back to the couch. It was abundantly clear that Edmund had something to do with Katelyn's death if he would treat strangers like that. "Let me guess... Katelyn tried to leave her just before he killed her."

"Right now, I don't have the evidence to say he killed her," Carson replied, a little strictly. "But... yes."

Maddie closed her eyes. "And the most recent victim... Carla was also trying to leave her husband, wasn't she?"

"She filed for divorce only two days before she went missing."

Maddie's thoughts whirled. Who could be so interested in killing women and their husbands once the couple had separated? Or was it something else? "Women in abusive situations are most likely to be killed when they try to leave."

"They are," Carson agreed.

Mike held up a hand. "But that doesn't explain who killed the husbands if they killed Katelyn and Carla."

Maddie shook her head. "Mike, you and I will go see Carla's parents. Carson, you stay here and have a nap. Understood?"

"I... all right," Carson grumbled. He settled himself deeper in the chair. "But be careful you two. From what I've seen, Carla's father wasn't any better than her husband."

CHAPTER
FOUR

NOBODY SEEMED to be home at the house of Carla's parents. The lawn and flowerbeds, which showed clear signs of being exquisitely cared for, were buried under autumn leaves.

Maddie rang the doorbell again, glancing at Mike. His expression was grim; his forehead furrowed slightly. When he caught Maddie looking at him, he attempted to smooth out his expression. He had a dark theory about what was happening here but hoped he could be proven wrong.

"The car is in the driveway," Maddie said. She knocked loudly on the door. "They have to be home."

"Maybe they went for a walk, or perhaps they have two cars and took one somewhere," Mike said.

But he still didn't believe that was the case. When Maddie peered through one of the side windows, he left the porch and rounded the building.

"Where are you doing?" she asked, following.

"You wait at the door in case someone answers," he told her, waving her back.

Continuing, Mike soon came to a window. He peered inside to find the inside in perfect order. Whoever took care of the house did a thorough job of it. Everything looked like it was out of a magazine rather than a home people lived in.

He knocked at the window and waited. When there was no answer, he rounded the corner and went into the backyard. He found the sliding glass door leading to the back patio ajar.

Mike took a moment to consider his choices. He could get himself, Maddie, and Carson into deep trouble if he went into this house without permission.

On the other hand, if he was right, there was evidence in here that needed to be found, the sooner, the better. And even if Carson came here right then, he'd have to get permission to enter the house. Every minute that passed meant the killer was getting further away.

Mike pulled a handkerchief from his pocket and found a single spot high on the screen door to push it open, careful not to touch anything. "Hello?" he called.

His voice echoed back to him. Hesitating a moment longer, he stepped inside.

Two steps in, and he had a clear view of the kitchen.... And the body that lay on the floor. Mike stopped where he was, his hands clenching at his sides.

He could be alive, he thought, and slowly made his way forward. He stepped into the doorframe leading to the kitchen, and the sight before him made his stomach lurch. Quickly, he retreated to the cool, clean air of the outside.

"Maddie," he called. "Back here—we need Carson."

CARLA'S MOTHER, Polly, had been killed by a blow to the back of the head. She was lying face-down on the kitchen floor. Based on rigidity and liver temp, the ME guessed she had been dead for over four hours.

Carson stared down at the body grimly. In the space of twenty-four hours, he now had five murders to solve. Even the captain, as much as he disliked Carson's methods, would not stand in his way.

"You really think your two writer friends will help you figure this out?" the captain asked, standing next to Carson in the kitchen, staring down at the body.

"You know I do; you've seen their work," Carson rolled his shoulders. "I need them. The force needs all the help they can get at this point."

"I unfortunately agree. But they are not to interfere with the crime scene, understood?" The captain glared at him until Carson nodded.

A shout came from upstairs, and Carson turned on his heel. He hurried away, the captain hot on his heels. They went into the bedroom as a young sergeant stood in the doorway. Carson recognized her; Adelayne, someone who hadn't been on the force for too long.

This would be her first murder case.

"What is it, Sergeant?" he asked, striding forward.

The captain lagged, silent.

"Sir. There's… well, another body." Adelayne took a deep breath and stepped through the doorway. "Male, mid-seventies by the appearance. Severe damage to the skull."

Carson stepped in. Just as Adelayne said, a second body was on the bed. Make that six, not five, murder victims found in the last forty-eight hours. This man lay on his face, still identifiable despite the damage to his skull.

"You may step outside if you need to, Sergeant," Carson said gently. "Get the ME up here."

The Sergeant nodded once and hurried off. Carson waited half a moment, but it didn't appear the captain was going to join him, so he pulled his tape recorder from his pocket and spoke into it as he observed the room.

"The victim appears to be Gordon Jordanson," he said, "he looks like the man in the pictures around the house. Heavy damage to the skull; at first glance, it appears to have the same damage pattern as the victim downstairs. The room appears untouched. No sign of a struggle."

He stepped around the bed, peering at everything intently. He turned off the recorder, not seeing anything further of note. His brow furrowed. How could someone have their head bashed in like that without putting up a struggle?

The ME came in, and within a few moments, the estimated time of death was the same as the woman downstairs.

Carson thanked him and left the forensic people to do their work while he headed downstairs. Mike and Maddie waited outside on the sidewalk, giving the police room to do their business. The captain was with them.

What is he doing? Carson thought as he headed over.

"Thank you, Captain," Mike said as Carson drew close. "We'll keep that in mind."

The captain looked over them, nodded as though satisfied, and walked off.

Mike and Maddie glanced at one another, rolled their eyes, and faced Carson. Neither of them looked very pleased, but they would have time to talk later about what the captain had said to them.

"Is it true, there's another body?" Maddie said.

"Yes. Another husband and wife, both murdered."

Maddie rocked back on her heels, a thoughtful look on her face. "Another abusive husband and battered wife if what the neighbors say is true. Mike and I talked to a few of them. The neighbor across the street, Sarah, said she heard a great deal of fighting from the house."

"I should talk with her, then," Carson said.

Mike stepped into his path, holding out both hands. "I don't think that's a good idea. As soon as she saw the police arrive, she closed everything up. It seems like she's afraid of talking to the police."

"I see." Carson glanced at the neighboring houses. If he was right, Sarah probably called the police on the loud arguments she'd heard, only for nothing to come of her concerns. He shook his head, glad he had two writer friends to help him get information. "What did she tell you about the couple?"

Maddie nodded at Mike, letting him take the lead. "She said that he was a huge bully. He took great pleasure in harassing the women on the street, so much so that everyone knew not to leave their houses at night."

"She knew him from middle school," Maddie added. "He liked beating up other children and stealing from them."

"So, a bully all his life, then?" Carson surmised.

Mike nodded. "That's what it sounds like."

"And their daughter was killed only hours before they were," Carson continued.

His eyebrows furrowed. He hated this sort of killing, but at least he had some connection to go from. Since four of the victims were related, there might have been a connection between the Hardings and them as we what sort of connection?

"These murders might be less the work of a serial killer and more the work of someone who has a personal motive," he murmured, thinking out loud. "If we can find a connection between all six...."

"I think we should look into the schools they all went to," Maddie said, arms folded over her chest like she was hugging herself. "The insanity of this is scaring me, Carson. But I really do think it has something to do with these men being abusive to their wives."

Carson agreed, but he couldn't figure it out for the life of him. He understood why someone would kill the men, but why would they also kill the women?

He put a hand on each of his young friends' shoulders, looking at them seriously. "I want you both to be extra careful. We've never dealt with a case where our killer was still at large and still killing. Don't let anyone into your homes without identifying them, and for goodness' sake, make sure all your doors and windows are locked—at all times. Understood?"

The last thing he wanted was for either of them to get hurt because of this investigation.

"We will," Maddie promised him. "And you keep yourself safe, too, okay? That includes eating and sleeping."

Carson gave her a fond smile. "Of course, Mother," he teased.

Maddie wrinkled her nose and stuck her tongue out at him.

"In the meantime," Carson continued, "there isn't anything else for you two to do here, and we should wait until we get forensics back before any more theorizing. Go home and get some rest."

Mike nodded. He slid an arm around Maddie's waist, and the two headed toward their vehicle. Carson watched them before he turned back to the house—there were answers; he knew it. He just had to find them.

CHAPTER
FIVE

MIKE SAT at his old typewriter, staring at the title of the book he had started a year ago and never finished. The plan he'd had for it remained vivid in his mind, yet even now, he couldn't seem to force the words out.

A knock broke through his thoughts, and he jumped. Internally scolding himself for getting startled over such a small thing, he went to the door. Maddie was coming over but remembering Carson's warning, he called through the door.

"Who is it?"

"It's Maddie, and I'm freezing my nose off! Let me in," Maddie answered.

Mike unlocked the door and opened it, welcoming her into his house. She hurried inside, bundled up in her normal sweatpants and oversized jacket. As soon as she was inside, she shed her layers.

"Ahh!" she sighed. "Out of that wind at last."

Mike cocked his head. The howl of an autumn wind outside gave the house a spooky vibe that would be perfect for writing his novel... if he could get into it.

Maddie hung up her outer layers and squinted at him. "Is there a reason you don't have any lights on?"

"Er… just got a lot on my mind, I guess," Mike replied. He turned on a few lights and led Maddie to the living room.

His furniture was a collection of cheap but comfortable things he found at second-hand stores or garage sales. Mike liked luxury in food, but for daily life, it was just a little too much to have fancy sofas. Even the wall art he'd hung around the place were pictures he'd picked up here and there, with no rhyme or reason other than he liked it.

Maddie's eyes fell onto his typewriter, and her eyes lit up. "Are you writing?"

"Not really." Mike closed the typewriter's case and moved it back to the shelf where it belonged. "I thought I would try to get some words out, but I haven't stopped thinking about this case. Not even writing can distract me."

"Oh."

Mike saw the worry in Maddie's eyes, and he winced. The last thing he wanted was to concern her. He smiled. "Don't worry; I'm still eating and sleeping. This isn't going to be like last year."

"I suppose it's been weighing heavy on my mind as well," Maddie said.

It had been three days since they had heard anything new about the case. They had asked around, searching for anything that could help Carson crack this thing. Unfortunately, all they had were theories for the time being.

"Maybe we need to talk about it, then," Maddie said bracingly. "A year ago, we tried to step back and let Carson handle the case and just focus on our own lives. If that will not work, then maybe we should let our imaginations run wild."

Mike laughed at the proposal. If there was anything he could safely say, it was that he and Maddie always let their imaginations run wild.

"They say if you can't beat them, join them," Maddie continued.

"Are you saying you will join me in this obsession because you can't beat it out of me?" Mike teased.

Maddie grinned and nodded. "That and Ben Hiddlestone is coming to town again in a few days. I want the three of us to bash out some good writing times, and we can't do that when we're hung up on this case."

Mike's mood lightened. Since he and Maddie had gotten to know Ben, the three of them had become good friends. He fit nicely into their writing partnership, adding some extra spice to his perspective.

Yes, it would be good to have this whole situation over and done with by the time Ben was here. Not that it was so easy to solve a case. But it gave Mike motivation beyond the obvious. He went to his record player, put on some classical music, and then paced around the living room. Maddie joined him, pumping her arms to get her blood flowing.

"Six people murdered. Three men, three women," Maddie started.

"All killed by a blow to the head," Mike added. "All with cases of domestic violence."

Maddie bumped into him, then stepped around him. "No trace of the killer in any of their homes. Forensic evidence shows the men were all killed by the same baseball bat."

"Unfortunately, baseball bats are difficult to trace, as they are largely made of the same materials."

Maddie hummed. "But the women weren't."

Mike nodded, stepping around Maddie. He faced her and walked backward, hoping it would spark something new in his brain.

"Carla's mother was killed by the same bat, but Carla and Katelyn don't have the same markings," Mike continued. It felt a little silly to repeat the information they already had, but at this point, they needed to find something new in the known. "Katelyn was killed by a blow to the front of the head against something with a sharp angle."

"And Carla has bruises down her side as though she fell down the stairs…." Maddie stopped walking suddenly.

She lifted her hands into the air; one held out to him to stop him from talking while she wrote in the air with her other one. Her lips moved silently as though she was talking to herself. Mike watched, his heart pounding shallowly. Had she figured something out?

"Katelyn's injury," she finally said. "As though she was thrown into the corner of a table or counter."

Mike frowned. "As though she was pushed into it, rather than something hit her head?"

Maddie rushed over to him and positioned themselves both next to the couch. "Pretend that the couch is a table. I'm Katelyn, and you're her husband. You're angry and abusive already and just found out I'm trying to leave you."

"I want you to stay here because I think of you as my property," Mike said.

"I say something that gets you furious—"

"And I hit you," Mike said.

He lifted one hand and mimed a slow punch. Maddie pretended as though he had hit her and stumbled back. She bumped into the couch and pitched forward as she turned to catch her balance. She tapped her head against the back of the couch, then got to the floor.

"Head wounds are deceptive," Mike said as he knelt beside her.

Maddie nodded. "There would be blood everywhere."

"Katelyn's husband might think he killed her, or maybe he would check her pulse and not be able to find it." Mike held his hand to Maddie and helped her back to her feet. "In any case, he doesn't want to call for help. His friend on the police force can only do so much."

"And covering up a murder isn't something he'd do," Maddie finished.

Mike shook his head, his eyes blazing. "And so he ditches Katelyn's body and reports her as missing. He plays the worried, grieving husband all the while knowing she's dead... and never has to face the consequences of his actions."

"Precisely," Maddie said.

"And Carla?"

Maddie positioned them both in front of the sofa again. "You're Carla, and I'm the husband. I'm angry because I just found out you're trying to leave me. We're standing in front of the stairs. I push you; I know that it'll hurt, but I also know that you won't dare tell anyone."

She lifted her hands and pantomimed a shove at his chest, not actually touching him.

Mike fell back, stiffening his body slightly, so his head hit the cushioned back of the couch. He imagined landing in such a way against a flight of stairs and winced.

"And again, it's a head injury. The blow killed her, so the husband, panicking, disposes of her body." Maddie paced again, her hands clasped behind her back. "Only someone had to know. Someone saw that Katelyn had been killed by a blow to the head and decided to kill her husband the same way."

"And then went after Carla's husband after it became clear that he killed his wife, as well," Mike murmured. "But why Carla's parents?"

Maddie tapped her lips with one finger. "Because they knew? Maybe because they told him where to find her after she tried to leave him?"

Mike hummed as he crossed his legs. "Her father was abusive toward her mother. A man like that wouldn't care so much that his daughter was being abused."

"And the mother could think that, since she put up with it, her daughter should as well. Maybe they taught Carla that it was her own doing, that she deserved it somehow." Maddie shivered. "That doesn't get us any closer on who would care so much about these women that they'd kill to avenge them, though."

"Yeah. It doesn't seem like Katelyn or Carla had friends. So who?" Mike stood again and went to the record player.

As he watched the record wind itself slowly in a circle, he thought back to when he was a teenager, and Mrs. Crabtree had gone missing. In his young mind, he had been confident that if her husband had been brought to justice, it would make him feel better about her death somehow…

Of course, it hadn't. The only thing that helped was time and learning to stop blaming himself.

"But what if our killer couldn't do that?" he said aloud, though he knew Maddie wouldn't understand what he was talking about. "What if the killer blames themselves for Katelyn and Carla's deaths?"

CHAPTER
SIX

WHEN CARSON ARRIVED at Mike's house early the following day, he found not one but two big corkboards sitting propped against the couch with dozens of newspaper clippings and articles printed from the internet pinned on them.

"I see you have been busy," he noted.

"The killer's name is Donovan Collins," Mike declared.

Carson's eyebrows rose. He had seen his young writer friends be confident with their deductions before... but had never had so much reason to doubt them.

The whole place was a wreck, unlike the meticulous Mike. Maddie sat perched on the back of a chair, pounding down a Red Bull while several other energy drinks lay on the surrounding floor. The table was covered with several meals' worth of takeout that had been eaten.

He frowned in worry at them. Maddie and Mike were slightly bloodshot, the sort of red-eyed look they got when they ended up staying up all night writing.

"Put that down," he said sharply when Maddie picked up another energy drink.

She dropped it, looking startled.

"We figured it out," Mike said. "Don't worry about the mess; I'll clean it up after I sleep."

Carson folded his arms. "You've both been up all night?"

Maddie and Mike glanced at one another, looking startled. It was as though neither of them realized what time it was. Carson rubbed his forehead.

"Maddie, get down from there. Both of you sit down and start trying to relax while you tell me what you figured out," Carson ordered.

Obediently, Mike sank into an armchair, and Maddie clambered down from her perch. She slumped back and yawned. Carson ensured they had no secret energy drinks around them and cleaned up the mess.

"All right. So, you think it's Donovan Collins," Carson said, monitoring them. He swept the empty food containers into a large black garbage bag. "Why would you think that?"

Mike straightened up some. "Twenty years ago, Donovan Collins was a twelve-year-old boy. His abusive father murdered his mother; the evidence was all there, and Donovan testified against his father, but for some reason, he was never convicted."

"Online rumor has it that Collins senior paid off the judge or perhaps blackmailed him," Maddie explained. "Anyway, the case was thrown out of court, and he was never brought to justice for killing his wife."

Mike nodded; his hands were clenched on his knees. "He was only a child, but the trauma of seeing his father kill his mother never left him. His father ended up locking him away in a psychiatric hospital...."

"Except he died two years ago," Maddie said.

Carson tied off the bag. "How could he have killed our victims if he died?"

"The father died, not the son. Donovan is still alive. But with his father's death, he no longer had the money to keep his room at the hospital and was released." Maddie nodded as though that explained it.

Mike cleared his throat. "Katelyn worked at the hospital. She would have become like a second mother to him. And when she went missing, he would have thought of his own mother, just like I thought of Mrs. Crabtree."

Carson finally finished his cleaning and came to look at the cork-boards. Every article had to do with the women's deaths; he frowned as he saw several printouts from online chat rooms.

"What's this?" he asked, pointing.

"We tracked down Donovan's various online presences," Maddie replied. "Since he spent so much of his life with his internet usage controlled, he didn't know how to protect his online identity. It was easy."

Mike stood and pulled one of the chat records off the board. "See this? He was researching ways to find a dead body. He claimed to be a writer and joined several writer's groups to ask."

"I've researched far more suspicious things," Maddie added. "Sometimes, as writers, we get into too much detail on this sort of thing."

Carson nodded once—he agreed with that statement.

"Anyway, Donovan was brutally abused by his father and saw his mother in these murdered women," Mike continued. "His experiences told him that the police wouldn't do anything, even if they had the evidence to convict their husbands."

"That isn't evidence."

Mike shook his head. "Read this. Just read it! It contains the exact details of these deaths. He got close to the husbands, found out what they did, and as soon as he was convinced that they had killed their wives, he killed them."

Maddie joined them. "Carla's parents remained in contact with her husband, even after she left him. I'm sure the phone records will show that they called him; they must have told him where to find her, and he abducted her."

"Abducted?"

"Yes. That's why she was in that getup, why there were bruises on her wrists." Maddie showed him another article. "Her husband wanted to control her and was keeping her a prisoner… perhaps even in her own parents' home. She must have tried to escape, and he pushed her down the stairs, killing her."

"So Donovan killed them, too, blaming them for Carla's death," Mike completed with a flourish.

Carson whistled through his teeth. "It's not evidence."

"No, it's not," Mike agreed. "But it's enough for you to find the evidence that you need."

It was a lead; that was right. More of a lead than Carson had had so far. He gathered the clippings and printings off the boards.

"Thank you," he said. "I'll take this to the captain. It might be enough for a search warrant. If Donovan Collins did kill those people, we'll find some evidence."

"The baseball bat," Maddie told him. "He was in Little Leagues when his mother was killed. He used that bat. He'll have kept it... for the next time."

Carson thanked them grimly. With any luck, they were right. And if they were, then he might prevent even more murders.

EPILOGUE

A MONTH LATER, Mike carried a full manuscript of a new novel within a binder tucked under his arm. The autumn leaves crunched underfoot as he walked up the drive to a rather large home. A dog barked behind the fence, that eager, joyful bark of a dog finding a new friend.

"Hello, Copper," he called as he stepped onto the porch.

Tricia answered the door almost before he rang the bell. She beamed at him, dressed in a blue apron. Flour dusted in her hair. "Come on in. The cookies are almost finished."

Mike entered the house. He'd been sure to take allergy medication before coming here to tolerate Copper's dander.

"Is that the book?" Tricia asked eagerly, eyeing the package under his arm.

"Yep," Mike replied. He followed Tricia into the kitchen. "Autumn Leaves. A Halloween story of mystery, danger, and paranormal thrills."

Since they had met that day, Mike and Tricia had become close friends. He enjoyed having another person to spend time with, and she had seamlessly entered the group with Maddie, Carson, and Ben Hiddlestone.

Game nights were exhilarating these days, as Tricia and Ben had competitive streaks that none of the others had.

She also had a tremendous love for horror, a genre Mike had little experience with that Maddie refused to read. Tricia would be invaluable as the first eyes to read his new novel.

Her kitchen was a disaster zone of flour, sugar, and baking supplies. Mike kept the edges so as not to dirty his clothes as he watched her finish plopping the cookie dough onto a baking sheet.

"I heard that the Collins trial was finished today," Tricia said, glancing at him. "That poor man... I couldn't bear to turn on the news and see if he was convicted."

Mike put his hands in his pockets. "He was found not responsible for his actions. He'll be treated in a psychiatric hospital for the rest of his life."

Tricia sighed. "I hope he finds some peace."

"As do I." Mike considered the case. It had been the most sobering one he'd ever been involved in... and yet, he felt lighter than he had in years. "Maddie and I plan to visit him from time to time. Hopefully, having people who care about him will help."

Tricia smiled at him as she put the cookies in the oven. "You're a good man, Mike."

"I certainly try to be." He beamed at her.

She blushed slightly, then wiped the flour off her hand. "Now. While those cook, let's have a look at this novel, shall we?"

Mike grinned. "Of course! Let's begin."

The End

MURDER AT THE RETREAT

PROLOGUE

DANIEL WINTERS carefully placed the thick manilla envelope at the bottom of his suitcase. His hands shook no matter how often he told himself to calm down. This would be the make or break of his career, so long as he played his cards right.

He swallowed thick salvia and placed his meticulously folded clothes over the envelope. Once it was hidden, the palpitations of his heart slowed down.

Make or break. This was his best work yet, his *magnum opus*. From this singular manuscript, he was going to achieve all his dreams. That was if certain other people saw the same things he did. He had been working on this for years now, chipping away at the story bit by bit. The whole thing was rather nerve-wracking.

Taking a few deep breaths, Daniel headed into his bathroom. A low, dull pain started in the center of his chest, and he grimaced, reaching first for his heart meds—he'd forgotten to take them this morning— and then the Tums.

He took one first, then the other, and washed them with a glass of water. Finally, he grabbed one of the new pills the herbalist had given him. He leaned his head back and dropped it into the back of his throat before drinking. This was the worst one. It smelled like a rat and tasted like sticking his tongue into a battery.

"Damn heartburn," he grumbled, massaging his chest with a trembling hand.

With another deep breath, he grabbed his bag containing a toothbrush, toothpaste, and a fresh bottle of Tums. After packing them, he glanced lovingly at his old typewriter. Too bad it wouldn't fit into the suitcase. Computer it was.

Zipping the suitcase shut, he hefted it in one hand and headed out of his apartment.

Portland, Oregon, here I come! Hope you're ready for me.

CHAPTER
ONE

MADELEINE MOREAU TOOK off her pale blue hat and placed it on the bed closest to the window. From here, she could see the Columbia River surrounded by the fragile green of fresh spring growth. Portland glittered in the afternoon sunshine. The hotels and apartment buildings lined the river, looking like little mountains.

"We've got a balcony," she said over her shoulder. "I want to wake up before dawn and sit out there wrapped up in a cozy blanket with a cup of coffee, watching the sunrise. We're even facing East, so it's possible."

Behind her, her writing partner and best friend chuckled. Mike was already putting his clothes in the bottom two drawers of the dresser on which the TV stood.

"You want to be outside before dawn?" he asked. "You, who are still wearing your winter coat?"

Maddie glanced down at herself. "This isn't a winter coat. It's a spring jacket."

"If you say so," Mike teased.

She rolled her eyes, grabbed her suitcase, and carried it to the dresser. Mike was finished putting his clothes away and headed out onto the balcony. As Maddie put away her clothes for the week that they'd be here, she couldn't stop a small stab of disappointment.

When Ben Hiddlestone, a fellow writer and Maddie's sort-of boyfriend (they went on dates but hadn't had the 'official' talk about what their relationship was), had brought up this writer's retreat, she had hoped that he'd be able to join her and Mike. Instead, he'd stayed home in Spokane. He told her and Mike to have fun.

Maddie had hoped that Ben would help her with this thriller mystery she had latched onto. Usually, she preferred things cozier. Ben was a well-known writer of mysterious thrillers, and Maddie had hoped to brainstorm with him.

Not to mention, she had planned to use this trip to figure out what their relationship was once and for all.

"Something wrong?" Mike asked her.

Maddie blinked and lifted her head. His brows were drawn together, a concerned frown on his face.

"Er..." Maddie shrugged. "I just wish we could have convinced Ben to come along."

Mike nodded. "Yeah, me too. It would have been awesome to have him. I guess he's got a point about only being able to write in solitude. But at least he, Trisha, and Carson have that hike planned. They won't be pining for our presence."

Maddie had to laugh at that.

Soon, her thoughts were turned to the retreat. They arrived a little later than they wanted and had to rush to prepare for the introduction luncheon. The retreat had only about twenty individuals participating this year so that everyone could sit at one table.

A middle-aged man with a thin, craggy face took the spot at the head of the table. He clinked his knife against his glass to get every-one's attention.

"Hello, everyone. Let's go around the table introducing ourselves, our writing backgrounds, and our aspirations," he said. "I'll go first. My name is Daniel Winters. I have published over twenty-seven true crime novels."

He grinned as he lifted his glass of water. His hand shook slightly, nearly making it spill.

"I'm currently working on an expose about a horrendous case

twenty years ago. I'm here to gather the last few details before sending my manuscript to my publisher."

The next person in line, a red-faced woman with lank brown hair, flushed an even deeper red. "Um. I'm Denise Foster. I haven't published anything yet, and I'm hoping to get, um, feedback on my novel. It's a romance."

She ducked her head, clearly embarrassed.

Maddie listened with interest to every person. They all sounded so interesting! When it was Mike's turn, he grinned at them all.

"My name is Michael Malison or Mike. I've been working for a few years as a ghostwriter. I've done some indie publishing as well. I'm here to gain new insights into other people's writing processes and hopefully make a few new friends. I mostly write mysteries but don't say no to reading or writing any genre."

"I'm Maddie," Maddie said. She left off her last name for now. She folded her hands in her lap as she smiled around the table. "I work with Mike closely. I'm more of a plotter. I love to create an intricate structure for books, but I don't have the patience to slog through chapter by chapter to find the perfect words. I'm here because I have a thriller mystery that I'm determined to write all the way through, and I'm hoping that the ambiance will help me stay focused."

The man sitting next to her made a bit of a harrumphing noise. "I'm Percy Morris. I write literary fiction. I'm here because my wife walked out on me."

He tossed back his glass of what Maddie hoped was apple juice. It was certainly too early in the day for him to be getting drunk.

The retreat coordinator, Lexi Black, took over as everyone started being served lunch. Evenings would be reserved for making connections. Every night, there would also be a draw from an anonymous first chapter for everyone to critique.

"I hope that you all have a delightful visit here," Lexi said as she smiled at all of them. "It will be a fun, exciting retreat."

"If I wanted excitement, I'd have gone to Disneyland," Percy grumbled.

Lexi gave him a brief, frustrated look. Maddie had to wonder how much he'd been moaning and grumbling already. She hoped they wouldn't have to spend too much time listening to him.

As much as she could sympathize with someone whose world got turned upside down, she didn't think this was the best way to deal with it. Then again, she wasn't sure how to react if someone she loved walked out on her.

"I'm going to pass around a sign-up sheet for anyone who wants to be part of the outlining critique," Lexi said, handing a clipboard to Daniel. "This is for those who are just starting and need feedback on the story's structure. It won't be anonymous, so ensure you've got your elephant hide on!"

Maddie laughed softly. Even though she loved plotting, this was certainly something she wanted to sign up for.

She wasn't having an easy time hitting the beats she wanted. The pacing of her thriller seemed off... rushed and too slow at the same time. Some feedback would certainly be helpful!

"So, Percy," Daniel said as he passed the sign-up sheet to Denise, "what's a *literary* writer doing here? Come to tell us all that our writing is derisive and formulaic?"

Percy barked out a laugh. "Yes, yes. All literary writers are snobs who write pretentious, depressing pieces. I subscribe to the belief that there is value in every genre... and that literary is genre work itself and people who try to say otherwise are bloated in their egos."

Daniel guffawed.

"Let's not get into any of that," Lexi said quickly. She looked nervously at Percy and Daniel. "We're all here to improve our writing, right?"

Daniel snorted. He muttered something under his breath but luckily didn't push it.

Maddie sighed. Good. The last thing she wanted was for this luncheon to get sucked into a debate. There were so many beautiful things to talk about!

She took a bite of her food and watched the various interactions around the table with interest. There were so many diverse personalities here!

It would be easy to incorporate some of these people into side characters for her novel. Maybe that was what she was missing. A rich cast of colorful people drives the plot forward. Maybe she was stuck because she used the plot to drive her characters rather than vice versa.

"Denise, what's your romance about?" Mike asked.

The red-faced woman blinked owlishly at him; her expression startled. From how she was hunched in her chair, Maddie could see she was trying her best to disappear.

"Um. It's about this girl. Well, woman. She moves to a small town to care for her grandfather after he breaks his leg. And then she meets the local doctor who is a..." Denise glanced down the table as though searching for someone to interrupt her. "A, um... Werewolf."

"So, a paranormal romance?" Maddie asked. She grinned at Denise as she took a bite of her sandwich.

Denise nodded.

"Love it," Mike said enthusiastically. "I'd love to hear more. Maybe you, me, and Maddie can go hang out at the pool and talk about it more later?"

Denise gave him an uncertain smile, her eyes flickering to Maddie. "Um, maybe."

"Or we could find that fire pit and have a fire," Maddie suggested.

Denise nodded, looking like she was trying not to be too excited. Maddie smiled warmly; Denise was painfully shy.

The sound of coughing caught her attention. She turned, then jumped to her feet, seeing Daniel's face turn purple. He grabbed his throat, a wild look in his eyes. Lexi was the first to him, pulling him up so she could try to dislodge whatever he was choking on.

"Call the hotel manager," Percy yelped.

Maddie whipped out her phone, calling 9-1-1. An operator answered, and Maddie described what was happening as Lexi tried to help. Daniel slumped to the table. Mike rushed over to give his help, too. Denise pressed both her hands to her mouth, eyes wide.

By the time the paramedics arrived, it was too late. Maddie stood with Denise and Lexi, feeling shell-shocked, as the paramedics took the body out of the room.

Daniel Winters was dead.

CHAPTER
TWO

"IT'S JUST AWFUL," Denise said. Her eyes were puffy and red, tears still trickling down her face.

Mike patted her shoulder, feeling that same weight on his chest. It wasn't every day you saw someone die right in front of you. He, Denise, and two other writers—Paul and Karla—were strolling along the path next to the Columbia River.

It was a beautiful, bright day. The freshness of spring filled the air with sweet scents, and birds sang mightily around them. None of them were paying much attention to it all. Denise had barely stopped crying.

"It's shocking, is what it is," Paul mumbled into his beard. His shoulders hunched. "I thought for sure he was choking. I thought he'd cough up whatever it was and be fine. I didn't even realize what was happening."

Mike turned to him. "I know. It's never easy to go through something like that. I'd urge you all to seek some trauma counselling. Because that is traumatic."

"Thank you," Denise said, sniffing. "I guess I should call my therapist. I live in town. I'll see if she'll have recommendations for everyone for the week at least... Guess I will not get any writing done anymore."

They arrived back at the hotel. The other three murmured to each other still. Karla said that there wasn't any point in just giving up on all the possibilities of the week and was encouraging Denise to at least try.

Mike only listened with half an ear. Several police cruisers were parked in front of the hotel. As they got inside, the other three split off toward the elevator.

"I'll catch up with you later," he told them.

Maddie's slim figure, dressed in an oversized sweater and thick tights, stood just outside the luncheon room where Daniel had died. Mike recognized by the hitch of her shoulders that she was watching something inside.

He trotted up to her. "What's happening?"

Maddie's expression was grim as she turned to him. "The medical examiner declared Daniel's death a murder. He didn't choke—he was poisoned."

Mike's shoulders tensed. Daniel had shown no signs of poisoning, at least not what he'd seen.

The detective walked over to them, a grim expression on his face. "I'm going to have to ask everyone in attendance to stay in Portland for the next few days."

Mike and Maddie nodded. They knew the drill.

"I'm going to have to ask you two to go back to your room now," the detective said. "Lexi Black will give me your information in case I need to contact you."

"Of course, Detective," Maddie said. "If we think of anything useful, we'll reach out to you at the precinct."

The detective eyed her but nodded. His expression didn't change, but somehow still grew more intense. Mike didn't like it. No doubt the detective thought it was weird that Maddie was hanging around like she had.

"Oh, there are a few things you should know before you look into us," he said. "You'll find that we've been involved in several murder cases in Spokane and one in Vancouver. But we weren't suspects. It's just that we were involved."

Maddie gave him a critical look. "You're allowed to say that the police asked us for help. We're good friends with Detective Carson Luttrell in Spokane."

Mike shook his head. "I didn't want to make it look like we were asking for an invitation into the investigation. That'd be weird."

"Oh." Maddie nodded. "Of course. We won't horn in; that's not how it works. Sorry. We'll just be going now if that's alright."

The detective hummed as he made a note in his notebook. "Please don't leave Portland."

His tone was dismissive. The two writers glanced at each other, shrugged, and headed for the elevator. Mike felt the weight of the detective's stare on the back of his neck. He tried to brush it off as they headed up to the room. Maddie folded her arms as she leaned against the side of the elevator, a pensive look on her face.

"What are you thinking?" Mike asked gently.

"That I thought was a murder. I'm trying to remember how everyone reacted. Lexi was the first person to think he was choking. Denise just sort of fell apart."

Mike shrugged. "Denise looks like she doesn't get out much. She seems like the kind to fall apart easily."

The elevator dinged open to their floor. They headed toward their room. Maddie was uncharacteristically quiet, that intense look still on her face. Mike touched her elbow, and she looked up, her gaze slightly unfocused.

"Hmm?" she asked.

"I think you might go through some trauma, too," Mike said, worried. "Let's see if we can find someone in town to discuss this. Normally, I'd say Carson, but I don't think it works so well over the telephone."

"I think we're all going to be going through some trauma," Maddie replied. "We saw someone die in front of us. But we're going to be fine. It's not like this is the first time something like this has happened. I just want to know why anyone would want to poison Daniel Winters."

Mike unlocked their room and held the door open for her.

Once inside, both kicked off their shoes and collapsed on their beds. Maddie had the one closer to the window, while Mike lay on the one closer to the bathroom. It was an unspoken agreement between them that this was what they always did when they shared a hotel room.

"I keep thinking about when he must have been poisoned," Maddie murmured. "It couldn't have been much before he died. For him to look like he was choking, it must have been in the meal we were eating."

"Unless he started choking because the poison kicked in."

"Are there any poisons that work like that?"

"I don't know, actually. I always use rare, quick-acting poisons in my stories."

They were quiet for a moment before Maddie rolled to her stomach and rested her chin on her hands. "Let's think about who had the opportunity."

Mike raised a brow at her. "We said we would not get involved?"

Maddie grinned at him, her eyes sparkling. "Oh, I don't mean to get involved. But all that writing advice is to write what you know, right? Well, this is the perfect setup for my thriller mystery. A small group of writers at a retreat, and one by one, they're getting picked off. Why? Of course, my story takes place on an island, so it's a closed circle."

"Are you sure you want to pretend this way?" Mike asked. "Don't you think it's a little insensitive to Daniel's death?"

"He wrote true crime. I looked him up while you were walking; he's the sort of guy who would start writing about the grisliest murders the day it happened. If it were any of us, he'd already start writing," Maddie advised.

"I suppose then he'd find it flattering."

"That's what I think."

Mike nodded. That made sense. "Denise was sitting on one side of him and Lexi on the other," he said.

"Ah, but Percy sat down after the drinks were poured and could have put something into Daniel's water," Maddie pointed out. "So there, we have three primary suspects. Lexi, Denise, and Percy. Daniel was being weirdly confrontational with Percy."

"Lexi is the one that set up the whole retreat," Mike said. "And Denise is just the sort of dark horse nobody would suspect. Her falling apart might just be an act. Or a guilty conscience."

Maddie grinned, clearly enjoying the challenge.

Mike shrugged off his concerns. Everyone dealt with trauma in different ways. Didn't he also like to turn fact into fiction so he could gain some distance from it? While working with Carson, they always went off into their spirals of plotting stories. The only difference now was that they had seen the crime take place.

Thinking of it that way, maybe he was the one that was being weird.

"What motive can they have, though?" he wondered aloud, trying to get into it. "Maybe Denise is his secret lover? And her romance book is about the two of them, and Daniel threatened to sue her?"

Maddie jumped to her feet, her eyes sparkling. "There's only one way to find out, isn't there? Let's go talk to her."

"What?" Mike rolled to a sitting position as Maddie rushed to where she'd left her shoes. "I thought we were still discussing the possibilities for your book."

"Yeah, but I need to get a better sense of who Denise is," Maddie argued. "You're the one who spent time with her after the luncheon. Let's see if we can pick apart what her novel actually is. She said it was a paranormal romance. I want to know more."

Mike lifted his hands. "What about Lexi? What could her motive be?"

Maddie hesitated, then took off her shoes again and returned to sit on her bed. "She's the one who organized the retreat. But we discovered it because of that newsletter in the ghostwriter's notice board. So, it was open to lots of people. She could have sent a direct invitation to Daniel. But then why…?"

"Maybe she's also a lover?"

Maddie wrinkled her nose, shaking her head. "No. No, she'd have to have a connection to one of the true crime stories he wrote. So, we should research the books he wrote and see what he submitted for the critique circles. See if any of that points to her."

"And that leaves Percy. His motive is obvious," Mike said with a grin. "He was insulted by Daniel at the luncheon, and it's a crime of passion."

"Or he meant to poison himself and accidentally got Daniel," Maddie pointed out. "Now. Who do we start with?"

CHAPTER
THREE

MADDIE SIPPED AT HER TEA, ankles tucked to one side under her armchair. She and Mike both sat across from Percy in his hotel room. They had decided that, since he was the least likely of all their suspects, it'd be best to start with him.

"I don't mind telling you, this whole death thing has unsettled me," Percy said. Unlike at the luncheon, he seemed sober now. "I tell you, I thought I would have time here to get out from under the shadow of my wife walking out on me. Now, it's like there's a whole unfamiliar shadow over me. Murder! Are you sure that detective said murder?"

Maddie nodded, keeping her expression neutral. "I'm afraid so. It was a mixture of hemlock and strychnine. Whoever did it certainly didn't want Daniel to survive."

Hemlock was common enough throughout Europe and the Mediterranean, but it had also been introduced into North America. It wasn't exactly tricky to find it, either.

Strychnine, on the other hand, was a compound that was processed from seeds of the *Stryphnos Nux-Vomica* tree. While the tree grew in India and Southeast Asia, the compound was used as a pesticide against small birds and rodents. Maddie didn't know any grocery store to carry it, but it couldn't be that difficult, either.

Percy's eyes widened. "Two poisons? Why would anyone want to do that? What do they do, anyway?"

"They're both alkaloids that act in the same ways," Mike replied, running a hand through his hair.

He'd worn 'casual' clothes for this interview. Meaning he looked like he belonged on the cover of a magazine. A dark blue sweater that hugged his torso and complimented his dark hair and eyes combined with a pair of black slacks. His expression was distracted, though.

"Both are paralytics," Maddie said. "And they target the respiratory system. That's why it looked like he was choking. His lungs had stopped working. The terrifying thing is if Lexi had given him mouth-to-mouth instead of trying to save him from choking, he might have pulled through."

Percy shuddered. "Any idea how long it takes to activate?"

"The hemlock takes anywhere between half an hour to several hours. Strychnine, when ingested, takes about fifteen minutes. So, it had to have been administered just when the meal started. The introductions took about fifteen minutes," Maddie said.

Percy shuddered again. "Then it must be that Lexi or Denise, doesn't it? They're the ones that were sitting right next to him."

"Did you see them touch his glass or food at all? Can you think of any reason they'd want him dead?" Maddie prompted.

"No," he replied.

"If you were to make up a reason?" she asked. "Like, maybe Denise and Lexi were both having affairs with him."

Percy gave her a startled look. "Why would you say that?"

She gave him a small smile. "Sorry. I'm sure the police will handle it, too. But the way I process trauma is to turn it into my fiction. I'm actually trying to approach this like I would a story. I'll never publish it, but I'm writing it into a story."

Mike's expression was frustrated, but she tried not to overthink that.

Percy shook his head slowly. "Well... I guess just before everyone else arrived, I saw Lexi talking with him. She seemed upset, and when I was refilling my drink, I heard her say something about it being not his story to share."

"Not his story," Maddie repeated softly under her breath. What did that mean? She could think of many things.

Now, though, she needed to get a lot sneakier with her questioning. Asking about other people was one thing. This? Something else entirely.

She nudged Mike's ankle with her toes, using the excuse to cross her legs the other way to do so.

"Do you mind if I use your bathroom?" Mike asked, standing.

"Go right ahead. There's a candle in there if you need it," Percy added.

Mike slipped into the bathroom, leaving Maddie and Percy alone.

She sighed heavily, putting on an air of sadness. Working undercover was her favorite thing to do, and this was just an extension of that. "I'm sorry that I didn't get to know him better. I thought that as a true crime novelist, he could have done me a world of good."

"I wouldn't count on it," Percy said with a snort. "Trust me."

"Oh? Did you know him?"

Percy made a face as though he'd said more than he wanted. "We met before at a writer's retreat last year. I took my wife with me because she was writing a nice little cozy mystery. She thought the same thing. Maybe Daniel Winters would be useful to get some tips from."

"Did she cheat on you with him?" Maddie gasped, her eyes widening.

"What? No! Nothing of the sort. My wife, or ex-wife, whatever the case might be now, would never do that. She was never one to sneak around. She walked out on me, but that was because I was too stubborn to make a few simple changes... and it's too late now. She's been asking me for years to think more about her and..." Percy trailed off, his shoulders slumping.

Maddie studied him in silence. He seemed to be genuine. "I'm sorry. I didn't mean to jump to the worst conclusions."

"It's fine. Winters was a very... charismatic fellow. He stole my wife's manuscript. She let him have a copy, and next thing we know, he published it under one of his pen names." Percy grunted and shook his head.

"He had pen names?" Maddie asked in surprise.

"Sure did. He wrote under the names of Summer Daniels—not brilliant, I'll tell you that—as well as Danny Hunter. I looked into him a great deal, hoping to help my wife with her lawsuit against him. Look up *Moosejaw Murders* by Summer Daniels. That's my wife's writing, word for word."

"It must have been a tremendous shock to come to this retreat and see his face," Maddie said sympathetically.

Percy snorted. "It sure was! The bloke is lucky that I didn't get drunk enough to confront him. Did you hear that crack to me about literary fiction? It was like he was trying to turn all of you against me!"

"It was so unnecessary," Maddie agreed.

"He's lucky," Percy repeated. "If I'd gotten my hands on him, I'd have—"

He cut himself off, his eyes widening. Maddie tried to keep her expression neutral. He'd pushed too hard, and now she needed to ensure he didn't think she thought anything of it.

"Well, I'm sure that it'll be easier for your wife to get her due royalties now," Maddie said.

Percy stood. "Why would I care about her now? She walked out on me. I did all that work for her, and she just up and left."

Maddie thought about pointing out that just minutes ago, he was talking about how he'd seen it coming for years. But that seemed too cruel. Instead, she stood as well. "Of course. I'm not sure what I was thinking. Mike's been in that bathroom a long time—I better make sure he's okay."

Percy squinted at her, suspicion on his face.

She knocked on the bathroom door, and a few moments later, the toilet flushed. Mike came out, rubbing his stomach. He grimaced as though he was in pain.

"I'd stay out of there for a while if I were you," he said to Percy, then to Maddie. "I need to get back to the room."

Maddie nodded in sympathy. "Thank you for talking to us, Percy. Hopefully, the police take care of this ugly matter soon."

She and Mike headed out and toward their room. It was getting late in the day, almost supper time. They'd arranged to take their meal with Lexi but had about half an hour before they needed to get ready.

Once they were in their room, Mike shook his head. "He doesn't have any medications that I saw. Certainly, nothing that would have hemlock or strychnine in it."

"That was a long shot, anyway," Maddie said, crossing the room.

The view of the Columbia River looked especially beautiful from here. She watched as it lazily flowed through the city and tried to piece together what they had learned.

"Percy had the motive to kill Daniel if he was trying to win his wife back. I really believed him when he said it was too late. I think he recognizes where he went wrong and that the grand gestures aren't enough; his wife needed him a million different ways, and he disappointed her too often," she said.

"That's the feeling I got, too." Mike joined her. "I thought he was too open about everything he said to have been a killer. Even with your charms disarming him."

"Yeah, and why would he decide to kill the man when they still haven't exhausted their legal actions?" Maddie wondered aloud.

"It makes little sense," Mike agreed. "Besides, I was thinking about it more. Hemlock has an unpleasant smell to it, and both it and strychnine are bitter-tasting. Why didn't he smell it? Taste it? It can't have been in his water. It would have been too obvious."

Maddie scratched her head thoughtfully as she considered the problem. "He had that onion soup he was eating. It would have masked the scent and smell."

"Speaking of," Mike said, glancing at his watch, "we'd better come up with our plan for how we're going to tackle Lexi. Any ideas?"

Maddie laughed. "I certainly do!"

CHAPTER
FOUR

THE HOTEL RESTAURANT was practically empty. No wonder, considering that it was earlier the same day that Daniel had been poisoned. Mike had to admit he had his own doubts. What if it was a random kitchen staff who'd poisoned his food?

Mike knew that the chances of that were so unlikely as to be nearly impossible. No, whoever killed Daniel Winters had been targeting him specifically and had been at the luncheon.

"I did everything I could," Lexi said, poking at her food.

She'd ordered mashed potatoes and a chicken breast; it was unlikely for poison to hide in there. It was why Mike had ordered off the kid's menu; the blander the food, the more likely he'd taste anything off about it. Maddie had ordered a decadent-smelling mushroom ravioli that was making Mike wish he'd ordered something tastier.

"You did," Maddie agreed with a nod. "Nobody could have known that he wasn't choking."

"But he was," Lexi said.

Mike raised his eyebrows. "The detective told us he was poisoned."

"He was. Oh, I'm getting mixed up." Lexi rubbed her forehead. "What I mean is, he was poisoned, but he was choking, too. I saw something go flying from his mouth right before he collapsed. I'm sure of it."

"Huh. So… the poison took effect at the same time as he choked?" Maddie wondered aloud. "Maybe he realized what was happening and tried to stop himself? And then that's all it took to weaken his lungs enough to make the poison kill him so quickly."

Lexi laid down her fork. "That's what the detective told me. I'm just so unsettled by all of this. I've known Daniel since I was a little girl."

"Oh? How did you meet?"

"My mother was murdered."

Mike winced. "Oh. I'm so sorry."

"It's alright. She wasn't ever really in my life. A socialite who was always drinking and partying. The cops never solved her case… nobody cared." A soft smile spread over Lexi's face. "Not until Daniel showed up, that is. You know, before he wrote true crime, he was the best investigative reporter there was."

"Yeah, I know," Maddie said with a nod. "I've been reading about him. He seemed like he was quite the colorful character."

"He was." Lexi laughed. "I begged him to come on this retreat. He was taking a vacation over in Greece and kept telling me there was no reason for him to return to the state. But he came."

Mike cut one of his chicken nuggets in half. He'd ordered plain water with his meal and was starting to really think twice about it all. There was lobster fettucine on the menu. And the wine list! He could have gotten the finest wine from Italy. Instead, it was like he was five years old on the family farm, eating the most boring food ever to exist.

Ah, well. He was complaining about the upset digestive system today. Tomorrow, he'd go all-out on the finery that was here.

"You know, he's the one that put me through university," Lexi continued. "He didn't have to, but he paid for all my classes. I never would have been able to get to where I am without him. And now he's gone. Poisoned! Just when…"

"Just when what?" Maddie asked.

Lexi shook her head. "Just when he was helping me with my debut novel."

"Percy told us he stole a novel to publish under a pen name," Maddie said. "I find it hard to believe."

Lexi clenched her fists on the table, her eyes fiery. "Percy is a drunk! Daniel Winters never stole a single word from someone else!"

"But he said—" Maddie started.

"Maddie," Mike said in a warning tone. He gave her a significant look. "You know what? I actually left my wallet up in the room. It's got my key card in it. Do you mind…?"

Maddie glanced at her ravioli and pushed it toward him. "Finish this; the hotel will charge it all to the room, anyway. I'm not feeling up to dinner after all. Just text me when you're heading up, and I'll be waiting to let you in."

She pushed away from the table and headed off, her shoulders slumped and head hanging low.

"I have to apologize to her," Mike said in a low voice. "She handles this sort of thing differently than most people. She meant nothing by it."

It was all going according to their plan. Of course, they hadn't known who would leave the table beforehand; they needed to know who Lexi would be more open to first.

"Maybe not, but it was very rude," Lexi muttered. "Daniel wouldn't have taken anybody's work and passed it off as his own. He wasn't that sort of person. He was kind. Why do you think he wrote true crime? Because he wanted to make sure those victims were never forgotten or written off."

"I never could read his work myself, but I've heard many good things."

"He was brilliant," Lexi said fervently. "And he still had so much to give. The saddest part of all of this is that the detective told me that the poison wouldn't have killed him if he hadn't choked. Oh, and because of his other medications. He could have finished his book."

Mike made a note of these details. What medications was Daniel on? What sort of medication would lead to the hemlock and strychnine killing him if the poison alone wasn't enough? Had the killer intended for him to take more, and he hadn't because he choked, or was it because the killer hadn't put enough in his food?

"This must be very difficult for you," he said. He put a hand on Lexi's. "Especially since you just had that fight."

Lexi looked startled. "Fight?"

"Someone heard you and him arguing about something... something being not his story to tell?" Mike shrugged and ducked his head like he was embarrassed. "I'm sorry—I shouldn't be listening to gossip and rumors!"

He sighed heavily as he speared a ravioli onto his fork and stuck it into his mouth. The sauce was thick and creamy, the flavor combinations making his chicken nuggets seem like dog food.

He could have wept at how wonderful it was.

"We did have a fight," Lexi whispered.

Right. He was trying to find out information—now was not the time to get lost in the beauty of food. "You did?"

Lexi nodded, looking ashamed of herself as tears collected in her eyelashes. "It was about his book. He let me read it... it was about me. Written from my perspective about my mom's murder."

"The expose he talked about."

"Yeah. There's so much detail in there that I told him about. I felt... violated. But he was trying to show a new angle to his work. How the crimes affect those left behind."

"But written as though it was you... that had to be raw and emotional," Mike said.

"It was stupid. I understand now what he was really doing." Lexi wiped her eyes, then pushed her food away. "I don't think I'm hungry."

Mike caught the server's eye and gestured them over. "Can we get to-go boxes, please?"

The server bobbed its head and left. They came back soon with the boxes, and Mike loaded up the food. Was there anything else he needed from Lexi?

"I hope you don't mind, but do you know what medications Daniel was on?" he asked, looking up. "It's just, I wonder if the poisoner knew."

"Heart medication and something for bronchitis, I think. He moved to Greece for his health. The climate agreed with him better," Lexi explained. She picked up her boxed leftovers and stood. "I'm sorry to leave so abruptly. I just want to be alone."

"Of course," Mike replied.

He gathered his own boxes but moved slower.

As soon as Lexi was out of sight, he ordered a second portion of the ravioli and a bottle of Riesling to be sent to the room, then headed back to Maddie.

She was on the computer when he got there, her expression intense.

"Daniel Winters suffered from heart problems and bronchitis," Mike said as he set the boxes of food down on the TV stand. "Apparently, it was a combination of choking, his medications, and the poison that killed him.

Maddie looked up. "What medications?"

"I don't know."

"Do you think we could get into his suite?" Maddie asked him.

Mike shook his head. "Not a chance."

"Hmmm. That's too bad."

He stuck the chicken nuggets into their mini fridge, and just a knock came on the door. He answered to find room service. They have him the second helping of ravioli and the bottle of wine he'd ordered. Mike thanked them, tipped them, and then brought them into the room.

Maddie shut her laptop. The two of them arranged a little space on an end table to eat at and sat down.

"Socrates was killed with hemlock," Maddie said as they ate. "But apparently, it was used for medicinal reasons, too. Some people use it to treat things like asthma."

Mike nodded. "There are a lot of poisons that, at the right dose, can be used as medication."

"It has nasty side effects even when it doesn't kill you, though."

"Like what?"

"Shaking. A burning sensation through your digestive tract, increased saliva, muscle pain, and weakness. Convulsions. Coma." Maddie shuddered. "If it weren't for the strychnine in there, too, I would have thought that the killer was actually trying to just make his life miserable."

It certainly would make it miserable.

"Did you learn anything about strychnine?" he asked.

"It might be what killed Alexander the Great."

Mike whistled. "Socrates on the one hand, Alexander the Great on the other. And he was in Greece. Wonder if it's a coincidence."

Maddie shrugged. "I don't think so. Pieces of this puzzle are missing... although I'll have you know, in my story, another of the writers has turned out missing. And they left behind a suicide note, but they're not dead... yet, at least."

"Really?" Mike asked, glad to be away from the macabre topic. "So, what's happening?"

Maddie grinned as she eagerly scooped up the food. "It started with the wine; you see..."

CHAPTER
FIVE

MADDIE SANK into the hot water, sighing in contentment. She hadn't even realized just how much tension she had been carrying in her body until the heat relaxed her muscles. She closed her eyes, letting her head lean back against the rim.

"Thanks for convincing me to come down here," Denise said from across the hot tub, where she sat near Mike. "I was going crazy in my room, circling repeatedly in my thoughts. I know I'm being dramatic, but I just can't stop wondering if there was something I could have done."

"Like what?" Mike asked.

"I thought something smelled off after Daniel finished introducing himself, but I didn't want to interrupt anyone else."

Maddie opened her eyes again. She watched Denise's chin sink to her chest, her eyes following the tiny bubbles as they floated back and forth over the surface of the water.

"Smelled something off? Like what?" Mike prodded.

"It smelled… mousy," Denise gagged. "I thought maybe something was wrong in the kitchen."

Maddie straightened. "Hemlock is said to have a mousy scent to it. But if you smelled it, then Daniel would have had to have it as well. I can't imagine he wouldn't have, especially after putting it into his mouth."

A look of confusion crossed Denise's face. "Do you really think so?"

"Yeah. Did you see anything weird before he started to choke?" Maddie asked.

Denise thought hard, a frown on her face. Slowly, she shook her head. "I wasn't paying attention to him. I was trying to memorize what everyone else was talking about so I could hold a conversation with them all later."

"Lexi says she thinks she saw something come out of his mouth before he passed out," Mike said. "Did you see something, then?"

Denise shook her head, looking ill. "No. I didn't see anything. I'm sorry. Can we talk about something else?"

She was panting, a look similar to panic in her eyes. Maddie winced. It was clear this was not good for her. How could someone like this be a cold-blooded killer? It didn't seem possible. Denise was just... so worried.

Sure, some people might say it was a guilty conscience, but Maddie thought it looked more like an anxiety disorder. Her heart reached out to Denise, wanting to help her navigate these anxieties better. She had mentioned that she had a therapist, and Maddie hoped it would help.

"Let's talk about something else," Mike said.

"Yes. How about our writing? I can't remember what you two said you were writing," Denise said, looking relieved.

"I'm currently working on an epic fantasy for a client. I ghostwrite for the most part," Mike said. "Usually, I like to work on mysteries, but right now, I've got a change of pace. I can't go into a great deal of detail for it; I was hoping to get involved in the writerly atmosphere here."

"And I'm working on a thriller mystery. But I don't think you'll want to talk about it. The basis is very similar to what happened here," Maddie admitted. "So similar, I probably won't end up publishing it. So far, everything I've written has been more of a... well, self-therapy, I guess you could say."

Denise frowned at her. "Why would you do that? I write the world how I want it to be; I can't imagine writing something so bleak as how the world is."

Maddie shrugged. "It helps me cope. But like I said, it probably will never be published. Not in its current form, at least."

"Have you published before?" Denise asked, scrunching her nose.

"Only indie publishing. I'm privileged to come from a wealthy family. So my writing is more about me expressing myself and wanting to bring entertainment to the world, rather than as a serious career." Maddie waved her hand under the water, watching as the top rippled. "I love my work as a ghostwriting plotter, though. I've gotten a lot of good feedback on that."

Denise chewed her lip. "I'm not very good at plotting."

"Neither am I," Mike laughed. He pulled himself out of the hot tub and sat on the ledge. "That's why I do my best work with Maddie here. We're a good team. She loves the plotting. I love the writing."

"You both seem so... glamourous," Denise sighed. "I don't think I have the confidence to be successful. My husband always tells me I need to believe in myself more. But I just look at writers like Danielle Steel or Jane Austen, and I know I'm not good enough."

Maddie reached across the spa to take Denise's hand. "You know who else isn't Danielle Steel or Jane Austen?"

Denise gave her a puzzled look.

"Nora Roberts. Julia Quinn. And Danielle Steel isn't Tessa Dare. That's the point." Maddie gave her an encouraging smile. "You're your own author, which is much better than being anyone else. Now. Let's hear about this paranormal romance you're writing. Maybe we can give a few pointers."

"I don't enjoy talking about it," Denise mumbled.

Mike hummed. "Do you want to just go over some of the basic points for a plot, then?"

"Sure. Maybe that will help!" Denise laughed. "I know how it starts; I know how it ends. But how does it get from point A to point B?"

Point A to point B. Of course! Maddie gasped. She got out of the hot tub and raced to where she left her towel and hotel robe.

"What happened?" Denise cried, startled. "What's wrong?"

"Nothing! I just realized—how did the poison get onto the plate?" Maddie said. She hurriedly toweled off her legs. "You weren't aware of the smell until everyone was introducing themselves. After Daniel did.

The food was served first! So how did the poison get from point A to point B, the plate?"

Denise's eyes were wide and confused as she watched Maddie. "Uh…"

"Maddie. Slow down. Talk to me," Mike said. "What did you figure out?"

Maddie pulled on the robe. Her skin was still damp, and the cloth did that gross squirming thing that happened with clothes on skin that weren't dried off enough. She ignored it with some difficulty. She needed to return to Lexi's room before the writer's retreat coordinator went to bed.

"I'm not sure," she hedged in reply to Mike's question. "I just realized something. And if I'm right, then it's going to change everything. I just hope I am right! Because otherwise, there's a killer among us!"

She dashed off, ignoring the startled protests from behind her. Mike called for her to wait, but she didn't slow down.

In her head, she imagined this moment for the protagonist of her book. Of course, Emmaline Guthered wouldn't be running to get the last piece of the puzzle—she would have realized that the killer was almost on their next victim. Such a thing wasn't happening to Maddie.

There was only one person the killer had been after… and Maddie wasn't so certain that they'd been trying to kill Daniel Winters, either. Nothing made sense at first, but now she saw it all so clearly in her mind.

The elevators were on the tallest floor, so Maddie dove through the doors leading to the stairs. Her robe came undone and flapped on either side of her, her one-piece bathing suit leaving water droplets in her wake.

Her protagonist would wear a bikini. Bright pink with flower details at the waist. It wouldn't be on purpose—she would have thought she packed a different swimsuit, but the flowers would give her the last clue.

Yes, the hemlock would be the poison there, just as it was here.

Maddie shook her head, banishing the thoughts of her book. She was panting by the time she reached the third floor. As she stumbled into the hall, the elevator chimed. She glanced over to see the doors open. Mike and Denise, both wearing their own hotel robes, rushed out when they saw her.

Heat rushed to Maddie's cheeks. She tried to regulate her breathing as she waited for them to catch up.

"What is going on?" Mike demanded.

Maddie swallowed and padded down the hallway. She explained as quickly as she could. "The key is in Daniel Winters' expose about the murder of Lexi's mother. He wrote it from Lexi's point of view, remember?"

Mike nodded, looking lost.

A surge of triumph went through Maddie. Usually, it was Mike being dramatic and making her wait for the answers. But this time, she figured it out first.

"He might have written it from her perspective, but it's still ultimately going to be his words. His story," Maddie explained as they got to Lexi's door. She knocked firmly. "And with these charges of plagiarism coming against him, he had to make sure that Lexi wouldn't claim his work, either."

"I am so lost," Denise said, looking bewildered.

Mike nodded his agreement.

The door opened. Lexi was wearing a set of plaid pajamas, her hair loose. When she saw the three of them, her eyes widened. "What's going on?"

"Do you still have a copy of Daniel's expose?" Maddie asked.

"Well, yes," Lexi said, looking even more bewildered. "Why?"

"I need a copy. The key to his killer is in those pages, I'm sure of it."

Lexi opened the door wider. "All I have is physical proof. I'm not letting it out of my room, but you can read it."

Maddie nodded her thanks as she came in. "Let's get to it, then!"

CHAPTER
SIX

DETECTIVE CARSON LUTTRELL smiled at his two young friends as they came to the climax of their story. He had to admit, he'd been engrossed in their retelling of the Daniel Winters case. He knew where they were going with this—he'd been contacted by Detective Beans in Portland about them—but Ben and Trisha were both on the edges of their seats.

"Oh, come on!" Ben groaned as Maddie took a long drink of water. "You can't just leave us hanging! What did you find?"

"First, it took us hours to read through that manuscript," Mike said. He swirled his cranberry juice in his wineglass, looking pensive. "It was worth it. So well written! It made me feel inadequate for sure."

Ben laughed. "Don't I know it! I read a bunch of Winters' stuff while I was researching my last book. The man could give Shakespeare a run for his money."

Trisha swatted his arm. "Noooo, don't distract them! Who was the killer?"

"In my book or in real life?" Maddie teased.

Trisha narrowed her eyes.

Maddie chuckled, then spread her hands. "It was in the pages of that manuscript we found our answers. Daniel Winters described himself as an odd, robust man who was too critical of doctors and put too much stock in new-age treatments. And that was how we got the answer."

Ben and Trisha both leaned forward. Carson took a long drink of his orange juice. It was nice that someone else could be the captive audience for a change. It would disappoint his young friends if he was the only one they could recount their dramatic tale to.

"What was the answer?" Ben breathed, his eyes not moving from Maddie's face.

"Daniel Winters killed himself."

Both Ben and Trisha audibly gasped. Trisha stared with a slack jaw while Ben's face twisted in concentration.

"He killed himself... because the only person who could put hemlock in his food was himself?" Ben asked slowly. "That's why the point A to point B discussion triggered something in your memory?"

Maddie nodded, smiling in a pleased sort of way. "Exactly. Only Lexi or Denise could have slipped something into his food while the rest of us weren't looking, but him? No. He'd have seen it."

"Not to mention he had to have smelled the hemlock before he ate anything," Mike added.

"Strychnine is odorless but, like Hemlock, has an extremely bitter taste," Maddie said. "Between the two of them, there's no way he would have missed it. So, it only leaves one answer. He introduced that poison himself and ate despite the smell and taste because he was expecting it."

"The detective found pills containing both hemlock and strychnine in his suitcase," Mike said.

Trisha leaned back in her chair, looking stunned. "He really killed himself. But why?"

"It wasn't on purpose. He was suffering from a weak heart and bronchitis," Maddie explained. "And while he was in Greece, he decided he didn't like the side effects of the medications his doctor prescribed him."

"He went online and started reading forums and sought an herbalist to give him the plants. He thought it would make him well again." Mike shook his head, sighing.

Carson shook his head as well. "It's a horrible way to go. A horrible thing for you all to witness, too."

Maddie tucked her long legs underneath herself, pulling her oversized sweater over her knees. "I noticed when he made his introduction, he was shaking. One symptom of hemlock poisoning is tremors."

"But how could he think that poisoning himself was a good way to cure himself?" Trisha asked, shaking her head.

"*Digitalis* is a heart medication derived from foxglove," Carson told her. "It's derived from foxglove, a deadly poison."

Maddie nodded. "Technically, the spice in things like chilis is a toxin, too. Historically, hemlock was used to treat respiratory illnesses, and strychnine was used to treat heart problems."

"So, what happened at the dinner, then? Why did it kill him if he'd been using it already?" Ben asked.

"The toxicology reports stated he had taken a double dose of his heart medications earlier that day. No doubt he'd forgotten that he already took it. Reading his manuscript, he portrayed himself as a much less likable character than Lexi thought of him," Maddie added.

Trisha frowned.

"The man in the book is self-aggrandizing," Maddie said. "But there was an undercurrent to it like he never truly believed in himself. Despite the success he had in his career, he didn't think he was all that great. It's clear he thought his reputation linked to that expose."

Carson drank more of his juice. "So, how does it link in with Percy's wife?"

Here, Mike chuckled. "She never shared her manuscript with her husband. She was secretly publishing under her own pen name, Summer Daniels. When Percy found out, she lied."

"She was building herself a nest egg to leave him. The whole thing was a lie," Maddie said.

"Wow."

Maddie nodded her agreement. "But with the lawsuit hanging over his head, Daniel was worried he'd end up in a similar situation with Lexi. So, he planned to slip himself a little hemlock. Just enough to make a scene at dinner so Lexi would feel badly toward him."

"That's what Maddie thinks," Mike interrupted. "I personally think he was planning on making overtures that Lexi was the one that poisoned him, so if she made a fuss about his manuscript, she would be viewed suspiciously."

"He cared about her, though."

"He cared more about himself."

Carson put his glass aside. "Now, that's not something either of you can say for sure. The man's dead, and whether it was malicious, a publicity stunt, or a simple mistake, we shouldn't dwell on it."

Both Mike and Maddie nodded.

They fell silent then; everyone lost in their own thoughts.

Eventually, Trisha stood. "Well, this has been very exciting. There's a lot to think about. But I've been here longer than I thought I would be. Copper is going to be worried about me."

Copper was Trisha's golden retriever.

"I'll walk you home," Mike volunteered, jumping to his feet. He gave Trisha a wide, flirtatious smile.

Carson hid his own smile. He was glad that their little circle had expanded. Having more close friends could only be a good thing— although the age difference between him and the others was becoming more and more obvious.

"I should head out, too. I have an early morning if I'm going to get these chapters written by my deadline," Ben said. He shook his head, clearly disappointed in himself. "Wish I could have been there with you."

Maddie grinned at him. "Next year."

The three headed out, and Maddie looked at Carson, lifting one of her perfectly groomed eyebrows.

"What?" he asked.

"Don't think I didn't see those faces you were making," Maddie said. "When did you figure out that Daniel Winters had accidentally killed himself?"

Carson laughed. "When Detective Beans called me and asked how much trouble he should expect from you and Mike?"

Maddie's jaw dropped. "He called you?"

"He certainly did! He had already figured out what had happened at that point. He just needed to wait for the toxicology report. But don't feel bad. Think about it this way: you didn't have nearly as much information as he did and followed your clues to the same conclusion."

Maddie wrinkled her nose. "I suppose."

"Not only that, but you have the perfect plot for your next book."

"You're right." Maddie leaned back into her chair, smirking. "It is the perfect plot. Now, all I have to do is write it. A spring writer's retreat, full of mystery and action."

"You could say," Carson said slowly, a sly grin crossing his face, "you need to *spring* into action!"

The End
Did you enjoy *the Mike and Maddie Mysteries?*
Please consider rating it on Bookbub or Goodreads and at your favorite retailer.
Reviews help me reach new readers.

Have you read the *Jane and Kennedy Daniels Mysteries*, the *Annie Archer Paranormal Mysteries*, *Wilma Wade Holiday Mysteries*, or the *Pine Grove Mysteries*?

Join my newsletter for writing updates, new releases, sales, monthly riddles, and more at www.daisylandishromance.com